To our friends

David & Pat

Renegade Gold

Kit Napier was a drunk despised by the good folk of Goldrush until an Indian uprising forced him to rediscover his lost skills as a scout for the army. It wasn't the Indians who started the war, rather those white men plotting to supply them with guns for payment in gold. But, once Kit has escaped his fate at the hands of the red men, that payment was destined to be made in blood.

In an unlikely partnership with a girl from the saloon, he fought both the renegade Indians and treacherous members of his own race. Would his desperate bid to prevent the territory going up in flames succeed?

Renegade Gold

ROBERT ANDERSON

A Black Horse Western

ROBERT HALE · LONDON

© Robert Anderson 2008
First published in Great Britain 2008

ISBN 978-0-7090-8547-8

Robert Hale Limited
Clerkenwell House
Clerkenwell Green
London EC1R 0HT

www.halebooks.com

Typeset by
Derek Doyle & Associates, Shaw Heath
Printed and bound in Great Britain by
Antony Rowe Limited, Wiltshire

For Katy and Ben,
and for Anna's unfailing encouragement.

CHAPTER ONE

THE TUSCATOON STAGE

Morning stirred softly and long, pale, pink-tinged fingers of sleepy dawn light began to steal over the bare, rocky slopes that spanned the far eastern horizon. Their slow beams reached out, arcing over the arid desert to pick out the sun-blanched, shingled roofs that marked the optimistically named township of Goldrush.

In point of fact the settlement had been populated for many years before it was ever so christened, or christened at all. It had seeded itself when the first wagon trains headed west, skirting the great desert that hung around its southern border. There was water in plenty to be found there, an important point when the great barrels that fed the trains hadn't been filled for weeks, and in due time one of the more enterprising of the would-be homesteaders set down his roots. He soon began to prosper and eventually established a general store and saloon to service the rapidly swelling trek to the far west. That investment seeded other small businesses and soon grew to accommodate a second saloon when the army moved in, constructing the compact little fort that stood a bare mile from the jumble of shacks that had grown around what had become the commercial centre of the town.

Gold fever struck when a lone prospector staggered out of the hills with dust in his poke, and for one, all too short season the town was inundated by an ill-equipped army of rag-tag would-be gold miners. In the event the settlement never lived up to the name it earned, for no more than one of their number ever made his fortune, a man lucky enough to stumble over a silver lode in his prospecting. Impatient for a share in the gold which was never found he sold out to a local mining company, who bought up his claim and secured a future in silver for the town already named Goldrush. Regular shipment of the precious ore from the mine ensured it could continue to support two saloons, a general store and a bank, besides enough houses to home the well-to-do and a regular shanty town of shacks for the mine workers.

In the main square in front of the bank, the stage to the rail head at Tuscatoon was set up ready to depart, furnishing a scene of unusual bustle for the time of day. A pasty-faced youth doggedly held on to a quartet of restless horses attached to the dark bulk of the coach, their breath forming tendrils of steaming condensation in the cold of a desert dawn, while nearby, two men buffed their arms to kick start their own circulation. It was a deceptive opening to the day and both of them knew it. On the edge of the desert, once the sun had risen into a cloudless sky the temperatures would begin to soar.

'Never thought to see you leave the army, Major.' Jake Lassiter, whip-cord slim in his leather jerkin and faded work denims, began to address a military man. His bright-eyed habit made a distinct contrast to the grey in his hair.

'High Command reckon I'm too old, Jake.' Major Monaghan, despite his enforced retirement, was still dressed in smart regimentals, as upright and ramrod straight as any of his junior officers. He paused for a moment as though considering the matter, and then sighed gustily. 'Perhaps they're right at that.' His voice echoed a hint of doubt, but he kept the bitter edge under strict control.

'Off to stay with your sister, I hear tell.'

'Alice,' confirmed the major. 'She's widowed so we'll keep each other company.' He stared off over the arid scrub land that ringed the town. 'I haven't seen her face to face in nigh on twenty years but we've always kept up a correspondence.' His face warmed. 'At least it'll be better than fighting Indians again.'

'I've lived around here as long as this town existed,' returned the driver easily, 'and I've never seen any more Indian trouble than a couple of young braves feeling their oats could raise.'

'It may be different this time, Jake.' The major spoke from a position of knowledge. 'There's a new chief speaking in the lodges. Pale Wolf they call him, and with good reason. He's calling for all out war against the white man and with dozens of new settlers streaming in to take the best land, that's a popular notion with the bolder spirits among them. He's involved in running guns too; in cahoots with a local man by the sound of it.'

'I heard that too. Modern repeating weapons they say, but I don't know any man living around here who would sell guns to the savages.'

'No more than a couple of rifles so far,' confirmed Major Monaghan, 'but if he can deliver in bulk, Pale Wolf will win the popular vote.' He shook his head sadly. 'Properly equipped and led by a chief able to unite them, there's more than enough Indians to sweep this entire territory clean before the army have time to react.'

'Sure can't be a local man then, or he'd be swept away with the rest,' decided Jake. A door rattled and both men turned their attention to the boarded sidewalk that ran along one side of the street. A solid timber door that led into the sheriff's office opened wide and a tall, rangy man dressed in badly stained buckskins staggered through followed by the bulky figure of the sheriff himself.

'I see Napier's been drinking again.' The major made no attempt to keep the disdain out of his voice when the figure shambled towards them still shadowed by his jailer. 'He was a good man until he hit the bottle. Scouted for the regiment when we were engaged in the Indian wars up north, but he's run to seed since those days.'

'Mr Hurst tells me the stage company want this here drunk for a guard.' The sheriff hauled his prisoner over to join them. Largo Baines, long term lawman in Goldrush, had a similar opinion of his charge to the major. 'God knows why; he'll probably be sleeping it off most of the way.' He jerked his head to indicate his contempt for the man. 'Couldn't hit a barn door in this condition!'

'Don't be too sure of that.' Jake Lassiter had known Kit Napier for many years and didn't scruple to disagree with the lawman's curt summing up. 'I never seen him miss what he shot at, that's for certain, and if this here Pale Wolf is half as bad as the major reckons, I for one will be glad to have him along.'

'Your funeral, Jake.' The sheriff shrugged his shoulders. 'All I need is a nod from the company's agent that they're willing to take him off my hands.'

'You have that from me,' assented Jake.

'What'd he do this time, Sheriff?' the major broke in to ask his own question.

'Black drunk; got into a fight when he was asked to leave the saloon. Laid out two of the hired muscle and smashed some of the fittings, but they tossed him out eventually. Straight into my arms! The cells stink of cheap booze and I'd have him clean them out this morning if the company hadn't offered to pay for the damage in return for his gun.' He threw

11

the gunbelt he carried across one shoulder at the dishevelled figure leaning against the coach.

Kit didn't seem to be in the mood to thank the sheriff, but for such a shambling, hung-over specimen he caught the belt with remarkable ease and buckled it smoothly around his waist. One huge hand then plucked the pistol from its holster to check its action with easy grace, while the other fed fresh rounds into its well-oiled mechanism.

'There's a rifle up top, Kit.' Jake Lassiter dismissed his new guard and turned his attention on the bank from which a small retinue had emerged. Mr Hurst, the manager, amply built and impeccably suited led the way at a stately walk, followed by two bare-chested blacks hauling a trolley on which the chests of silver bullion lay. Bringing up the rear, shotgun to the fore, Len Connors, the bank's principal security guard, strode out in their wake.

'Mr Hurst.' The driver tipped his hat politely when he greeted the manager. He was an important man in town and liked everyone to acknowledge that fact, more especially since he knew the stage line couldn't afford to operate without his contract. 'Need any help loading?'

They both knew the question to be rhetorical. The bank always did its own loading, but an air of politeness had to be maintained.

'No, thank you, Jake. The boys can take care of it. Major.' He inclined his head in recognition of the ex-army officer and stood quietly to one side while the sweating blacks manhandled the heavy boxes on to the stage and roped them securely. 'Keep your eye on them, Connors.'

Len Connors, a surly, rough-looking individual, had already taken up a position on the roof of the coach, his shotgun slung comfortably over one arm. 'Ain't no one getting hold of these 'til we get to Tuscatoon, Mr Hurst,' he growled.

'How many passengers today?' Mr Hurst blatantly ignored the guard, whom he fully expected to do his duty, and stared at the ill-assorted troupe trailing across the street towards the stage. 'Isn't that the storekeeper and his wife?'

'Mr and Mrs Armitage have just sold up,' confirmed Jake, tugging on his straggly beard. 'I hear they're planning a vacation way out East before they settle. The other fella's a drummer, name of Jeff Wright; he's been out trying to sell equipment to local farmers. Seen him supping in the saloon once or twice since I brought him in, but I ain't heard yet that he's made a sale.'

'What about the strumpet from the saloon?' Mr Hurst rudely butted into Jake's explanation, glaring angrily at the neatly dressed figure bringing up the rear. 'Is she on your waybill?'

'Miss Myers paid her money same as everyone else, Mr Hurst.'

'I'd rather she wasn't travelling on the stage while you're carrying silver bullion. A woman of her ilk knows all kinds of villains.' Having made his point, the bank manager conceded, resigned to the woman taking her place in the vehicle, though the sheriff was puzzled enough to pass his own remarks on the subject.

'I didn't realize she was leaving town today?' He stared at Jake for confirmation.

'Late booking,' the old man replied. 'She came down to the office yesterday evening just as we were shutting up.'

'Tallulah Myers.' The sheriff stared at the slim, neatly dressed figure in a scarlet travelling costume with a hard glint in his eyes. 'Heard tell she was Jem Horne's girl. What d'you think, Jake?' He looked to the driver again.

'Well,' replied that worthy easily, 'she's never had to rely on being a crib girl, that's for sure. Used to hang around Jem a lot too, but he's always done what he pleased with the other girls. Perhaps she got sick of his philandering ways and decided to move on. Hear tell she was an actress one time.'

'Good riddance,' decided the lawman at last, and stepped forward to help Mrs Armitage up to the stage door. She thanked him graciously, but flashed a look of indignation at the saloon girl who was following hard on her heels. Her husband had owned the general store and she wasn't used to mixing with women of that stamp. Jeff Wright had no such inhibitions however, and waved Tallulah forward politely, only to press in behind too close for her comfort.

'Get your damned hands off me,' she cried out in sudden outrage, scooting to one side and lashing out at him with a roundhouse slap that would have knocked him down if it connected.

The drummer only laughed and made another step in her direction, only to find the way blocked by Kit Napier, who'd leapt lightly from the vehicle, instantly putting to flight any suggestion the drink may have left him incapable. The salesman doubled his fists, openly contemptuous of the dishevelled guard, but Jake immediately stepped in to put an end to the argument.

'I wouldn't do that if'n I were you, Mr Wright,' he told the drummer quietly. 'This is one man it's best not to rile the morning after; he can act real mean after hanging one on.'

The drummer glared impotently at Kit, but was wise enough to take notice of the driver's advice and he climbed into the vehicle without taking any further action. Relieved to have defused a potentially dangerous situation, Jake stepped forward to offer Tallulah his arm.

'Climb aboard, Miss Myers,' he told her, 'we'll be off any minute.'

At the door she paused long enough to thank both men with a graciousness that surprised the old driver. Then, with an agility that belied his age, he clambered up to the high front seat where Kit had already settled himself once again, and took control of the reins from the young ostler.

'All aboard, Major.' He shouted out a warning to the military man who was still deep in discussion with the sheriff, and set off as soon as that worthy had entered the vehicle.

CHAPTER TWO

AN INTERRUPTED JOURNEY

Jake skilfully tooled the heavy wagon down Main Street and out of town. He took it slow on the first stage, in the knowledge there were no horses to be had in a full day's run. The road was easy so far as the escarpment, the going firm and barely rutted, so he fully expected to make good time without any need to exhaust the beasts.

'What d'you reckon to these tales of an Indian uprising?' Jake broke the silence to question his companion, a man whose knowledge of Indian affairs was widely respected by all those who knew him.

'That what the major tell you?'

'He did. Gave me the tip 'bout some ornery character named Pale Wolf. Some sort of war chief apparently, though I've never heard any Indian of that name around here. Reckons he's whipping them up in a frenzy for war.'

Kit nodded. 'I've heard the talk, but the local chiefs don't have the stomach for war, not with an army detachment camped out in their backyard. I don't know enough about Pale Wolf to make up my mind, but if he's come in from outside, he'll have mighty little influence around the camp-fire.'

'The major tells me he's promising them guns, modern repeating weapons.'

'That could swing the matter for him,' decided Kit, 'but he ain't delivered yet from all I've heard. Nor might he ever. One thing's certain, without delivering the guns to back up his play, he'll win no more than a few young bucks to his cause, and the army will soon gain the upper hand.'

'I thought you knew all the Indians around here?'

'I know most of those whose opinions matter,' decided the guard carefully. 'Pale Wolf hasn't been one of them until recently. He's still shrouded in mystery; first I heard tell of him was no more than a couple of weeks since.'

'Who'd supply the guns?' Jake decided Kit would know if anyone did; he still visited the lodges.

'There's no more than a handful of modern repeating weapons with the tribes as yet. My sources indicate Pale Wolf's armed a select band of support-ers and the rest are only promised. He might have brought them in himself.'

'You don't believe that.' Jake was sharp enough to interpolate the information from what Kit was saying.

'He's got an accomplice to back him up. A white man, or at best a half-breed; maybe local, perhaps even in Goldrush itself. Pale Wolf convinced the council of chiefs to gather together enough gold to pay for the guns to be shipped in, but they haven't arrived yet.'

'That why the army has patrols out in force?'

'Guess so.'

'They'll stop them,' declared Jake confidently. 'Pale Wolf can't deliver with the cavalry on his tail.'

Kit looked serious. 'He'll be one sick Indian if he doesn't. The tribes don't set as much store by gold as we do, but they do set a high standard of honesty amongst themselves and he'll be in trouble if he doesn't make good his promises now they've paid out.'

'Do the army know that too?'

'They know.' Kit didn't say how he knew.

'Funny thing that Tallulah should leave town so sudden.' Jake switched the subject to their late booked passenger.

The guard shrugged his shoulders. 'Not much of a life in Goldrush for her.'

'Jem Horne's woman they tell me.' The driver made the question sound more like a statement. Kit Napier spent a lot of his time in the saloon and Jake was sure he'd know the truth.

'She was,' the guard decided, after a moment's thought. 'Not that it cramped Jem's style over much. Don't believe they've been together for a while now.'

'What's she do for a living?'

'Makes herself useful around the saloon, I guess. Sings too; no Nelly Melba, but good enough for a bigger stage than Jem's. To be honest I don't know her at all well, she's not a woman to put herself forward.'

'Jem's not the sort of man to let someone sponge off him, not unless she's his woman.'

'Like I say, I don't know details, but when she gives an order the other girls jump. Barmen, too. Reckon she helps him manage the place. Needs it, the way he fools around.'

Conversation continued in a desultory fashion until early afternoon, by which time they were well into the long, hard climb up the escarpment that cut off Goldrush from the north. For many years the early settlers believed there was no way through the fierce rocky impasse for anything less handy than a mule, until a pair of prospectors discovered the narrow pass that wound snake-like between precipitous walls of virgin rock. The approach was made by a steep track, surrounded by cliffs that rapidly funnelled in on a vehicle, and it was here the sheriff caught up with them.

'You hear that?' Despite his age, Jake Lassiter was the first to hear the lawman bellow. He stood up on his box and peered over his shoulder at the mounted figure behind.

'Can you see who it is, Len?'

'Looks like Sheriff Baines to me, riding hard.' Connors had maintained a taciturn silence throughout the journey, but he made up for that with a running commentary on the rider's progress. 'You'd better pull over and wait for him; he might have fresh instructions from the bank.' Significantly, however, he held his shotgun more prominently. As the bank's principal guard he didn't intend to be caught napping; even lawmen as respectable as Largo Baines had been known to turn bad for a sight less than the silver they were packing.

'Hauling a spare mount as well.' The old driver drew the stagecoach to a halt and twisted his head to stare at the rapidly approaching lawman. 'Take the reins, Len.' Kit Napier had already leapt down to greet their pursuer and Jake followed suit as soon as he was assured the horses would be held.

'You're in an awful hurry, Sheriff.' Jake took the lead in questioning the man when he trotted up and swung from his horse.

'Hoped to catch you before the pass,' confirmed Largo Baines. 'I know the stage travels down the other side a deal faster than it climbs up and I have a warrant for one of your passengers. Sooner I get her back to jail the better.'

'What's up, Sheriff?' Major Monaghan was leaning precariously out of the stage door.

'Nothing to worry about, Major,' the sheriff interrupted his story to reassure the military man.

'You mentioned jail, Sheriff. What's up?' Kit cut to the chase.

'Jem Horne, the saloon keeper, was found dead this morning. Looks like he was murdered last evening; shot at close range with a small calibre pistol. Doc Hayes dug out the cartridge and told me it would suit the tiny guns carried by some women in their bags, small enough to conceal, but deadly close up. The sort of weapon a woman who spends her life working in a saloon might pack.'

'That why you're after Tallulah?'

'Partly.' Largo Baines began to explain himself. 'Then again, we found documentary evidence in his office that Horne had been supplying guns to the Indians. No absolute proof, but there was some suggestion a woman was involved as his accomplice. Under interrogation, one of the barmen confirmed he was often closeted in his office with such a person, but he didn't know who she was.' He finished, 'Apart from Mrs Armitage, who I've ruled out, Tallulah Myers is the only woman to leave town, and in a mighty hurry from what Jake said. Not only that, she was Jem's woman.'

'Haven't seen her with Jem in a while, Sheriff, and nor have you. He's well known as a womanizer; could have been closeted with anyone in town.'

'True enough, I suppose,' conceded the sheriff, 'but she's the only lead I've got up to now, and I'm not allowing her to run off anywhere. She doesn't have to be Jem's woman to be his accomplice. I'll take her and her luggage back to town.' He turned to Jake. 'I'll have to search the other baggage. The Indians paid in gold and it sure ain't to be found in town.'

'I'll inform the passengers and get it unloaded for

you, Sheriff. No need to disturb the bank's shipment, is there?'

'There sure isn't.' Len Connors joined the conversation from his perch on top of the vehicle. 'I don't have a key to the boxes anyway, and there's no way you're going to force them open while I've a breath left in my body.'

'No problem, Len,' the sheriff reassured him. 'Hold up there, Jake.' He turned to the driver who was already beginning to explain to the passengers what the hold up was about. 'Let Miss Myers out first.' He drew his gun as a precautionary measure and gave further instructions. 'Take her purse; she's likely got a gun in there, and search her while I cover you.'

'You hear that in there?' Jake Lassiter passed on the request and a moment later Tallulah Myers was ejected from the coach.

She stared at the gun in the sheriff's hand with a rueful smile on her face, and held out her purse to the old driver.

'Search her!'

'Sorry, ma'am.' Jake approached her diffidently, but she raised her arms as though resigned to the indignity. He tossed the purse to the sheriff and ran his hands hesitantly over her person, shaking his head when he found no weapons.

Largo Baines shook out the purse and watched the tiny gun fall out with a smile on his face. Still covering the woman with his pistol, he asked Kit to retrieve the weapon.

Kit did so, weighing it in his hand thoughtfully. He sniffed at the barrel and opened the chamber. 'It's loaded,' he confirmed, 'but I'd bet on my life it hasn't been fired recently.'

'You've got the wrong woman,' Tallulah told the sheriff shortly, dropping her arms. 'I've had that pistol in my purse for years, but I've never had to use it.'

'Save your explanations for the jury.' Largo Baines wasn't interested. 'Toss her luggage down first, Len,' he roared. 'I'll go through that before we disturb the rest.'

Nothing incriminating was found in Tallulah's bags however, and by the time the remainder of the luggage had been unloaded for searching, all the male passengers had alighted and were relaxing in the shade cast on the lee of the vehicle watching the sheriff's thorough search of their baggage.

Thus no one was ready when the Indian war party attacked. The surprise attack was made by a small party of braves who'd approached on foot under cover of the rocky scree that covered the slopes around the track. Out of the coach, the white men were sitting ducks and it was pure chance that more damage wasn't done by the first volley of shots that rang out a moment before they charged.

CHAPTER THREE

INDIAN TROUBLE

Kit was the first to react, the air of alcohol-induced lethargy that enveloped him disappearing in a rush of adrenalin. He was already dropping into the dubious cover of the piled up luggage when his arm caught Tallulah, dragging her down beside him. The rifle, hanging negligently from one hand while he stood, was up and firing by the time he hit the ground. Under such circumstances there was no opportunity to aim with any accuracy, he fired only to encourage the advancing tribesmen to seek cover themselves and thus gain enough time to assess the situation.

The sheriff had acted almost as quickly, seeking the same cover, while the driver, with a moan of pain dragged himself awkwardly behind a particularly large trunk owned by the Armitages.

'You OK, Jake?' Kit, though he was aware of the driver's injury, didn't take his eyes off the rock-strewn slopes where the Indian war party had taken cover. He snapped off another quick shot to keep their heads down while his colleague replied.

'Been hit worse, son.' The strain in his voice was evident, however, and Kit risked a glance at his drawn, pale expression.

'I'll look after him.' Tallulah's calm tones soothed Kit's anxiety, and allowed the guard to resume his appraisal of their circumstances without worrying over much about his comrade's condition.

The sheriff, shifting his position to peer down the trail, swore bitterly at the loss of his horses. They'd both bolted at the first shot, tearing their loosely tied reins from the stage, but had stopped short a few hundred yards down the track when the gunfire quietened. 'Damn it. Those savages'll steal them animals for sure.'

'We won't be here to care if we don't find better cover.' Jake hissed in pain when the saloon girl began to work on him. 'Damn it, woman, what in tarnation are you doing to me?'

'You're losing a lot of blood from that wound,' she pronounced with bitter determination. 'I could let you bleed to death, but we'll need your help to stave off those savages and if I don't staunch the flow, you'll soon be too weak to be of any use.' She lifted her skirts and began to tear at her petticoats to provide material for the bandages she'd need.

Satisfied the old driver was being looked after despite his protestations, Kit turned his attention to the nearby coach. The normally calm horses had thrown themselves into a frenzy at the first fusillade and dragged the coach a dozen or so yards further despite the brake that held the wheels firm. The dead weight of the vehicle had proved too much for their strength, but they'd barely quietened and the guard knew it would take little or nothing to panic the poor beasts. Len was still on top of the vehicle, evidently lying flat, probably under cover of the silver chests, though he could be heard shuffling about.

The three men who'd left the confines of the cabin to shelter from the fierce sun in the lee of the stage, had tracked the vehicle's movement and taken cover beside the huge wheels. Mr Armitage was evidently wounded, for one arm hung loose while the sleeve to his jacket ran red with blood. Both he and the drummer had taken up a position at the rear wheel, closest to the group under cover of the luggage, while the major flattened himself against the front, peering around the driver's box to pick out the danger. All three had handguns out ready for action. Mrs Armitage was nowhere to be seen, presumably still sheltering inside the coach.

'How is he?' Kit directed his question to Tallulah who, having secured sufficient wadding from her petticoats, had wrenched open the driver's jacket and vest to reach the wound.

'Bloody,' she replied calmly. 'The shell's torn a gash in his side and maybe cracked a rib or two, but he'll live unless those Indians get hold of him.' Jake moaned out loud when she yanked hard on the makeshift bandage, tightening it across the wound, but he accepted her ministrations without complaint until another fusillade of shots burst out and the Indian tribesmen attempted another rush.

This time the party was ready and returned fire fiercely enough to drive them back immediately.

'No more than a half a dozen,' counted Kit dispassionately, 'and armed with single-shot rifles judging from the time between volleys.'

'I make it about that,' the sheriff agreed easily. 'They're wearing war paint, so we're not just a target of convenience.' He stared hard at the saloon girl who was still working on the driver's wound. 'The way this attack was planned, I reckon they already know they've been double-crossed; must have been after her, or their stash of gold.' The slightest of movements caught his eye and he pointed towards his horses which had nervously retreated even further down the trail following the resumption of hostilities. 'Couple more of the varmints down there after the animals. Nothing I can do about it; they're well out of pistol range.' He nodded meaningfully at the rifle held firmly in Kit's possession.

'I'll take a shot at them if they break cover,' promised the guard, 'but I reckon they'll drive the horses out of range before they chance it.'

As if to collaborate his statement the Indians began a high-pitched whooping that sent the nervous animals skittering further away from the beleaguered companions, until they were lost to sight where the trail curved around a taller outcrop of the rocky escarpment.

'Lost them.' Before the sheriff could expand on his theme, the crack of a whip and shouts of encouragement from the opposite direction grabbed all their attention.

Len Connors, keenly aware of the vulnerability of his special charge, had slid into the driver's seat, yanked off the brake and whipped the horses into motion. Already spooked, they threw themselves into the traces with an enthusiasm that jerked the stage forward before any of those in its lee had time to prepare. In his haste to save the silver, Len was willing to risk the lives of the remaining passengers.

'What the devil!' Jake dragged himself up to watch when the stage took off. A high-pitched scream marked the moment one huge wheel rolled across the drummer's back, cut off in its prime when his lungs were crushed under the vehicle's weight. Mr Armitage, left out in the open, sat open-mouthed in surprise and died when a murderous barrage of fire broke out from the ranks of the Indian foe, cutting him down before he had a chance to join his companions behind the luggage. The major, from his forward position, had more time to react, and he managed to grab a hold on the moving vehicle and hang on while Len attempted to make a run for it.

Those left alive watched in fascination while the tragedy unfolded. Escape looked possible for no more than a few seconds when, whooping and firing on the run, a further party of five Indians, this time on horseback, spewed out on to the trail ahead. The fleeing bank guard desperately tried to pull his team around, but, hit in the hail of lead, dropped the reins and toppled slowly off the vehicle. The major was as aware of the danger as anyone, and released his precarious hold to run for the cover of a nearby outcrop.

Everyone, including the attacking Indians, ceased hostilities to watch the end. Without a driver in control, and the horses galloping in terrified haste, the stage ran no more than another thirty yards before it ploughed into the rocks, reared into the air and overturned amongst the plunging steeds that drew it with a terrible crash. Even the major, still out in the open, stared at the dreadful spectacle for a moment, before remembering he was in imminent danger himself, and sprinted the final few yards to cover.

The mounted Indians raced in to set free the horses and gallop off with them, but the drama wasn't yet over. Mrs Armitage had somehow managed to survive the dreadful crash and appeared through the narrow doorway, now on top of the vehicle. With the savage attackers fully occupied in stealing horseflesh, against all the odds she somehow scrambled out and began to limp painfully towards her companions and safety, dragging one leg uselessly behind her. Another triumphant whoop, and a brightly painted brave was on her trail, whipping up his horse to run her down. Kit snapped off a shot, but the deed was already done, the Indian's feather-decorated lance thrusting through her at almost the same moment he too fell. Mrs Armitage was all too clearly dead, but the Indian rolled, lithe as a frightened jack-rabbit, into the same cover the major had taken.

The remaining four mounted braves, perceiving they were within effective range, retreated hastily with the three captured horses, leaving the last animal pinned under a corner of the wrecked stage-coach, shrieking in pain and fear. Kit took careful aim and put it out of its misery. Silence returned to the scene while the stand-off developed.

'I'd give my pension to know what them varmints are planning,' the sheriff iterated to no one in particular.

'I'll lay odds they'll work their way up the bluff yonder,' replied Jake. His voice still reflected the pain of his injury, but to Kit's immense relief some colour was beginning to return to his face. 'They're all armed with rifles of one sort or another. Thank God they're not all repeaters, or we'd be dead by now, not that it'll make much difference if they climb up higher. Kit's the only one with any more than a handgun, and God only knows if the major's got even that.'

They all eyed the bluffs speculatively, instinctively knowing the driver was right. Once their attackers had taken up a position above them, their position would swiftly become untenable. The luggage amongst which they were pinned down lacked the height to shield them from that angle.

'The major's taken cover in a good position,' Kit remarked, having taken stock of the situation. 'Next time they fire a volley we'll make a run for it. Are you up to it?'

He directed his question particularly towards the injured driver, who nodded his head in assent. 'I can still run if it's either that or die,' he confirmed.

'Two hundred yards at least,' estimated the sheriff, 'and it don't take much to reload. Even if we sprint they'll catch us on open ground. Jake's not up to travelling too fast, and neither's the lady.'

'We've got to risk that if it's our only chance,' Tallulah broke in. 'If you two help Jake, I can lift my skirts and run as fast as any of you.'

'I'll help Jake,' agreed the sheriff. 'Kit's got the rifle; he'll need to cover us if them horsemen take a hand. I don't fancy getting run down the same as Mrs Armitage.'

'Get ready to move as soon as they start firing,' warned Kit. 'If we want a volley, I'd better provide a target.' So saying he rose on his heels, and leapt out of the ring of luggage that covered them, ducking and weaving in a circuitous route that ended with a roll and a dive behind a small heap of shale. The first two shots whistled by while he was still moving, three more striking up spurts of dust alongside the shale that partly obscured his shrinking body. 'Go,' he screamed, and rolled several times sideways, knowing at least one of their enemy still had a shot to fire.

Tallulah was as good as her word; holding her petticoats high, she sprinted in a flurry of bare-legged athleticism towards the major's position, closely followed by Jake and the sheriff. The driver winced with every step, but eschewed any attempts by the sheriff to aid him and ran as fast as the rest of them despite the pain of his wound.

The major himself, understanding their predicament, opened up a brisk fire with his pistol to keep their enemies occupied, while Kit retreated watchfully in their wake. The last Indian fired wildly, caught between tracking Kit's erratic movement and his fleeing companions, and no one ever knew just where his shot went. Then, as they approached safety, their plans began to go wrong.

Neither the Indians reloading or those mounted had interfered, but they'd forgotten the single wounded brave who'd killed Mrs Armitage. Hit, but not incapacitated, he'd evidently been intent on stalking the major himself, and when Tallulah reached the edge of the rocky outcrop he leapt up and dragged her down.

Jake and the sheriff were a dozen yards behind, but too involved with their own escape to mark the saloon girl's fate, and the Indian promptly disappeared with his prize into the jumble of rock. Only Kit had noted the circumstances of the girl's disappearance and, oblivious to the flying lead from their attackers' reloaded weapons, he flung himself after her, only to find the girl and her adversary in a deadly scramble.

The two of them were jammed tight in a crevice barely big enough for one. Tallulah had both hands occupied in holding off the brave's knife, a wickedly sharp length of steel with a tooled bone handle. He, in the meantime, had hooked his free arm around her throat and was attempting to strangle her, hindered either by his wound or the narrow confines of the crevice. Kit leapt in to help, but Tallulah had the Indian's measure and, somehow managing to evade his crippling neck lock, contrived to get her teeth into his knife arm at the wrist. He yelled out loud and cuffed her, but she clamped her teeth together and hung on, his blood flowing freely through her mouth. It was nip and tuck as to whether the crunch of Kit's boot on his fingers or the saloon girl's sharp teeth caused the brave to drop his weapon, but he wasn't finished yet.

While Tallulah wriggled agilely from his loosened grasp, he strove to face his more dangerous adversary, diving at Kit's legs to bring him down. The stage guard had no intention of fighting in the confined space of the crevice, however, and he shifted ground far enough to evade the Indian's clumsy lunge.

A guttural curse and the Indian transferred his attention to the knife he'd lost, beating the saloon girl's desperate dive by a short head. This time he slashed, opening a bright pool of blood on her arm, then went for Kit in a scything, last ditch attempt to win his freedom and deny the white man time to shoot. Kit met the vicious attack with a two-handed hold on his rifle that blocked the bright steel, then hooked the barrel to beat the brave back.

Stunned by the blow and half blinded by the waves of blood pouring from the jagged wound opened on his forehead, the Indian stepped back and dropped his guard long enough for Kit to level his barrel on the weakened foe. The explosion echoed loudly around the rocks and the Indian finally succumbed, dropping where he stood.

'Thank you.' Tallulah sank down weakly in a jumble of frothing petticoats and shapely limbs, trembling in the aftermath of danger, but still managing to keep her voice clear. 'You could have left me to die. I thought I was a goner and that's a fact. There's not many men around these parts who'd consider me worth the effort of saving.' She closed her eyes and shuddered, hit by the sudden realization of how close she'd come to death.

'There's not many who'd consider me worth anything at all,' Kit returned briefly. 'How's your arm?'

The girl glanced at the ragged sleeve of her blood-stained dress and grimaced. 'It's painful, but really it's no more than a nick. Barely bleeding now.'

'Bind it up,' advised the guard. 'We're not out of danger yet, and you don't want it to open up again.' He reached out a hand to help her up. 'Come on, we'll join the others.'

Tallulah had been so involved in her own struggles she'd barely noticed the sporadic gunfire that showed the battle was still going on. She grasped the proffered hand and found a curious sense of safety in Kit's strong grip, despite his rumpled appearance.

CHAPTER FOUR

BREAKING OUT

Locating their companions was an easy matter. The major had justified his military status in choosing a rock-strewn knoll close against the precipitous cliffs of the escarpment as his fortress. It rose above the surrounding shale and boulder slopes, offering a perfect defensive position to the beleaguered companions. Reaching them while still under fire was a different matter.

Traversing the open slopes while remaining hidden from their savage attackers engendered a good deal of the sort of crawling and snake-like wriggling that a lady's travelling dress wasn't designed to stand up to. By the time the two of them had reached that safe fastness, Tallulah's own attire was quite as reprehensible as Kit's. Though she made no complaint, the delicate hue of the elegant costume was barely identifiable through the ground-in dirt and the stained material itself was rent in several places.

'Glad to see you,' the major greeted gutturally while levelling his pistol on a fleetingly seen target. 'We're keeping them at bay, but we badly need that rifle of yours. These pistols won't do much good until those goddamned savages work up the nerve to close in on us.' He turned to Tallulah and touched his hat respectfully. 'Thank God you made it, ma'am.'

Kit took his place on the firing line and quickly snapped off a couple of shots that had their painted assailants leaping for cover. They were congregating at extreme range for a handgun, but facing a rifle at that same distance was a different matter.

'I think you winged one.' Major Monaghan congratulated Kit on his immediate success. 'Least ways you'll have scotched their willingness to attack us face on.'

'What will they do now?' The sheriff's deep voice addressed the question to Kit. Notwithstanding his predilection for alcohol, they all knew and respected his knowledge of Indian behaviour.

'Wait until dark, I'd guess.' Kit stared around him at their position, assessing just how difficult it would be to defend against an attack at night.

'I thought Indians didn't fight at night,' put in Jake Lassiter. ' 'Case their spirits can't find the promised land.'

'Some tribes might think like that, but not any of those I know. Indians are mostly just like us,' explained Kit. 'They don't like to fight at night because it's harder to identify friend or foe. Can't see where they're going either, much harder to move around silently. Lots of reasons why it's better to fight in daylight.'

'Why wait, then?' Tallulah asked the question.

'We have far too good a defensive position up here and they're only a small war party. A full frontal assault is their only option right now, but it'd be suicidal to try and rush us during daylight, they'd take too many casualties. A night attack would be a different matter, they'd be able to creep up on us and launch the assault from close by.'

'Can we stop them?'

'Easily,' Kit made his opinion known. 'Unless another party is drawn in by the noise to reinforce them, there's no more than a dozen warriors in total. So long as we stay awake they won't take us by surprise and there's four of us here, well armed, and in good cover.'

'Five.' Tallulah surprised them all by holding up a stubby little gun she'd taken from her clothing. 'I retrieved this when the Indians attacked, Sheriff. You were too concerned with your horses to notice. It's no use while they keep their distance, but I'm told it's deadly close up.'

Kit nodded. 'We'll take casualties, but so far as fire power is concerned I reckon we can hold them at bay if we stay.'

'If we stay?' The major stared at the stage guard.

'There's nothing to drink up here,' explained Kit. 'Unless anyone thought to collect their canteen before they took cover, we'll soon start to suffer from the effects of thirst. Without water we'll rapidly become too weak to defend ourselves whatever those savages decide to do. Even if we do beat them back, there'd be more than enough left to ensure we remain holed up. During daylight hours, at least.'

'How do we escape?' The major surveyed their position, paying especial attention to the steep cliffs behind.

'There's no escape that way, major. Those cliffs would be hell to climb in full daylight, let alone by moonlight with a pack of painted warriors using you for target practice.'

'We can't just walk out!'

'Not yet,' responded Kit warily. 'Tonight. There's a moon later, but it's relatively new and only rises an hour or so after the setting sun. When it gets dark I'll light out myself; make enough noise to convince those savages we're all escaping, then lead them a dance to give you enough time to leave.'

'What if they continue to keep us under surveillance?' The major voiced his anxiety.

'They'll follow,' Kit replied steadily. 'I'll make sure of that, even if I have to twist their tails a bit, but unless their leader's a complete fool, I'd expect him to assign at least one of his braves to keep a watch on our position.' He paused a moment before adding a warning rider, 'You'll have to slip out in complete silence while it's still dark, but don't go too far before the moon rises. You'll get nowhere without its light to guide you.'

'It's a long trek back down the trail to Goldrush, especially if we've got a pack of Indians to out-pace.

Don't know that we'd make it what with Jake bad wounded and a lady along with us,' the sheriff broke in on the conversation, his gaze assessing the condition of his companions with pessimism clear in his tone.

'You wouldn't make it,' agreed Kit. 'The Indians would run you down soon as they got on your trail, but there's a farm close by where the Livingstone family live. I've met the old man in town once or twice.' He gave a wry grin. 'He liked to while away an hour or two in the saloon while his wife searched through the store.'

'It'll be easier to walk into Goldrush than hike all the way out to their place,' exploded the sheriff. 'The Livingstone place is situated way out on the old prospector's track that begins just beyond city limits.'

'It's no more than a dozen miles across country from here,' Kit insisted knowledgeably, 'and it may confuse our enemies long enough for us to steal a march on them.' He surveyed his companions with a steady gaze. 'It's a rough track to tackle on foot, but we can make it in a day's hard walk.' Then he stared forbiddingly at Tallulah's footwear. 'Frippery like that won't last.'

The saloon girl stared ruefully at her feet. Her shoes were little more than fashionable slippers and already showed signs of wear from her recent scramble. 'I have boots in my luggage,' she declared defiantly, 'and I'd be wearing them if I'd known I'd be taking a hike across country. These will just have to last.'

Kit shrugged. 'So long as you keep up. We'll all be dead if those Indians catch us in the open.'

The sun set early in the mountains and in the last throes of twilight Kit gave his orders. 'You'll have to leave soon after you hear me attempting to fool those Indians. They'll probably send someone up straight away to check whether we're all gone, so you'll have to move quickly, and for God's sake keep it quiet. You won't stand a chance against warriors like these in the dark. We'll meet at the old miner's shack, no more than a mile back down the trail.'

'I know it,' Jake broke in, 'almost a complete ruin. No roof and precious little height to the walls either. Won't those red varmints know about it as well?'

'They will, but as long as they don't realize we're set to rendezvous there it doesn't matter. Whatever you do, keep off the trail and stay close to any cover you can find. When you reach your destination, hunker down low and stay quiet. When they realize they've been tricked these savages are going to be mad as hornets.'

'Won't they follow our tracks?' The major's voice rang calm, but he was voicing all their fears.

'If they can,' confirmed Kit, 'but it'll still be night even when the moon rises. If you're careful enough it'll take some tracker to follow you in the dark over such rocky terrain. Daylight's a different matter; almost any Indian's good at tracking, but we'll be well clear of the vicinity by then.'

'If I don't make it to the ruins by midnight, head

due east, keeping off the skyline, and you ought to cut the old prospector's track some time tomorrow. They'll be after you by first light if not before, so don't wait around. Once you're safely ensconced in the farmhouse, it'll take a bigger party than this to winkle you out.

'Remember to wait at the ruin for me until midnight.' And with that final admonition Kit wriggled noiselessly out of their rocky fortress, determined to lead their attackers astray.

For several minutes not a sound was heard. Then the scrape of a boot sliding on loose shale echoed across the battlefield, followed by a muttered curse, hastily bitten off.

Kit moved fast once he'd alerted their enemy to his presence. As he well knew, one or more of them could lie hidden no more than a few yards away, and he hoped he'd left enough evidence to convince them a party had passed in the dark. Working his way further off the course his companions would be taking on their way to the rendezvous, he deliberately slipped again, this time letting his rifle ring out against the boulder under which he'd taken cover. He followed it up with a muttered order to keep it quiet, and slipped noiselessly away from his position, listening carefully to see if he could track the progress of the Indians who'd undoubtedly be searching for him by now.

He detected no sound in the quiet of the night, but didn't allow himself to be fooled by that. They'd be on the hunt for him even if they'd left a guard on his companions' position. Another artlessly careless chink from his rifle barrel led them further astray, and a few minutes later he received his first confirmation the Indians were on to him. For the briefest of moments a savage head was outlined against the lighter patch that defined the sky, barely visible, but uncomfortably close. Kit burrowed deep under another boulder and went to earth, keenly aware he was unlikely to be detected before the moon arose.

Half an hour later he rose again, satisfied from the lack of battle sounds that his companions had escaped unobserved from their beleaguered position. Scouting down the rocky slopes carefully, he came at last to the remains of the wrecked stagecoach, and with one final check on the slopes around him, slipped out into the open and the scattered chests that marked the spot they'd first made their stand against the savage foe.

He knew it was a high risk venture, for the moon, such as it was, was already beginning to rise and threatening to flood the scene with a spectral, if somewhat meagre, light. Nevertheless, Tallulah's boots were in her luggage, and he had to find them. Her flimsy footwear would soon give out and even if she could still walk on lacerated and bruised feet, the trail of blood would very likely be picked up by Indian trackers, even in the tricky light of a new moon. With both a wounded man and a woman in the party, they'd need every yard of the lead he hoped to win by his stratagems.

In the event, all went well, and by the time the

faint illumination provided by the new moon really began to make its presence felt he was reunited with his companions.

Tallulah, who'd already dispensed with her petticoats and cut short her dress so its hem hung raggedly around the trim curves of her calves, took the boots with a nod of her head, knowing better than to thank him out loud. With any luck they were a mile or so from the nearest Indian, but that couldn't be guaranteed and the scout motioned for them all to maintain silence when he led them out of the ruins and began the long tramp eastward towards the Livingstone farm.

In the maze of shadowed defiles and hanging valleys through which Kit led the tiny party, the light of the new moon barely helped, merely providing dappled patches of lighter gloom through which they hurried with fresh trepidation in case they were discovered by their enemies. It wasn't until the early hours that Kit felt they were far enough ahead of their savage pursuers to risk speaking, and then it was only to egg them on to even greater speed.

'There's a steep climb ahead,' he warned them, still keeping his voice low, 'but it's generally downhill after that. How are you, Jake?' He and the major had been supporting the old driver for the past few miles and he knew the old man was approaching the limits of his endurance. The woman too was reeling on her feet, and the sheriff wasn't in much better condition. Years of more sedentary living than was good for him had left him seriously out of condition, but the scout knew the wounded driver was the one who would most likely hold them back.

'I've been better.' Jake's voice broke under the strain of his journey. 'You ought to leave me here. If those varmints have a mind to chase us I still have enough vim left in me to plug a couple before they get me.'

'There's no need for you to play the hero,' Kit replied. He had no intention of leaving the old driver, the nearest thing to a friend he had left. 'If they'd managed to cut our tracks, they'd be up with us by now.' He pointed out the cliff ahead. 'It's a stiff climb, but if we make it to the top we're due a rest.'

'Tarnation.' Jake Lassiter let vent his feelings, and collapsed in a heap when he finally made it to the top of the cliff that barred their path. The major had shimmied up the vertical incline first to establish a bridgehead, quickly followed by the saloon girl, girding her skirts up to her waist and climbing agilely, her progress marked by the faint sheen of ivory skin, barely outlined by the fading light of the new moon. The sheriff and Kit reserved themselves to support the wounded driver over the most difficult parts of the ascent.

'Help me,' Kit swiftly requested the others. 'We've got to get him off the skyline.'

'How is he?' Once they were off the hill the scout selected a new position from which he could watch the trail behind, while the others took a well-earned rest. Tallulah made the driver as comfortable as

44

possible before joining him to make her report, but she wasn't optimistic about his condition.

'He needs more than a short rest; that wound of his would knock up a much younger man, let alone one having to hike across rough country. How much further have we got to go?'

'Four, five hours,' replied the scout. 'Fast walking pace, too.' He backed out of his position just under the crest of the hill where she'd joined him, carefully avoiding the risk of showing himself against the rapidly lightening sky towards the east. 'There's a stand of pine further along,' he pointed down the slopes. 'I'll make up a stretcher.'

The girl from the saloon rose to her feet with him. 'Thank you,' she told him awkwardly. 'For the boots, I mean. Well, everything really. We'd all be dead by now if you hadn't been with us.'

'The boots were necessary.' He spoke harshly, all too aware that no one had needed to thank him for anything recently. He hated the drunk he'd become as much as any of his old acquaintances, but he couldn't help himself. He was being rude and ungracious, he knew, but he couldn't take it and strode out of their makeshift camp in a savage mood, unaware he'd left the woman feeling she'd been snubbed again because of her profession.

He was away for more than an hour, but when he returned, he'd laced together enough brushwood on a sturdy pine frame to fashion a usable stretcher for the driver. Jake, he was anxious to see, had deteriorated even further and was able to do no more than mumble a few words of thanks, too sick and feverish to offer again to remain in an effort to hold back the savages that would be following in their tracks.

'We'll wait for daylight before we carry on,' he decided abruptly. 'A couple of hours' more rest will do us all good and it'll be easier carrying the stretcher. I'll take the watch.' Grim-faced, he strode off again, to guard their path from the Indians on their trail.

Kit had been right in his optimistic view that their route lay downhill, and in the fresh morning light the way was easier, just as well since the three men were now carrying the wounded driver. Tallulah had attempted to join them in supporting his weight, but she'd been too short to balance the load properly and they'd continued with Kit holding the rear on his own, while the major and Largo Baines took the lead, with the saloon girl's fading strength adding whatever aid she could give on the more difficult stretches. It was a slow journey and when they eventually made it to the outskirts of the Livingstone farm evening was beginning to fall. Here they sank to the ground in fresh despair when a sudden volley of shots rang out.

The Livingstones themselves were under attack!

CHAPTER 5

OUT OF THE FRYING PAN

'They beat us here after all,' the sheriff complained bitterly.

'Keep your head down, they haven't seen us yet,' warned Kit. 'Nobody beat us here either; this must be a fresh bunch. There's more than a score of the devils, still on horseback too. They've just arrived, or we'd have heard the sounds of battle way off.' He stiffened and raised his head higher. 'Caught at least one of the family outside.'

The truth to his assertions became all too plain when the cabin door opened and a woman began a rapid fire aimed at the horsemen milling around one of the nearer outbuildings. A moment later a frail-looking old man slipped out from a hidden position behind the shed and began to sprint raggedly across the open yard. The woman staggered and went down just before he reached the door and flung himself through it, dragging her inert body in with him. The door slammed shut again and the watchers breathed a sigh of relief.

'That was old man Livingstone,' the sheriff told them unnecessarily. 'We'd better get down there to help; he's a sick man, with no one but his wife and daughter to aid him.'

'Wait.' Kit was watching the behaviour of the Indians bunched around the outbuildings. 'There's someone else holed up in one of the barns trying to dodge them. Must be one of the women. Look up there!' His voice grew hoarse in the heat of the moment, for the slim figure of a girl had suddenly appeared in the open-ended loft to the biggest of the barns, and disappeared as quickly when she realized she was in plain sight of the attacking band of Indian braves who immediately began to whoop in gleeful anticipation of her capture.

'Come on,' Kit called. 'We'll never get another chance as good as this.' So saying, he heaved Jake's slumped figure over his shoulder and began to run determinedly towards the cabin with his bemused companions trailing in his wake.

The scout's bold tactic worked; the Indians were still directing all their energy to cornering the Livingstone girl in the barn, and in the gathering gloom it wasn't until the exhausted group were hammering on the door itself that any of them were noticed. The door opened and Livingstone himself greeted them.

'Thank God,' he prayed, and stood back while they filed swiftly in under renewed fire. 'Those devils have my daughter Belinda, holed up out there. She's been off staying at the line shack for a few days, only returned tonight.' He winced suddenly as though in fresh pain, and turned even paler than he'd looked at first glimpse. 'Took a bullet in the gut,' he admitted, and clutched at his middle where blood was oozing steadily through his overalls. 'They've hit Mary; don't know how bad, haven't had a chance to take a look at her yet.'

'She's dead!' Tallulah's stricken face looked up from the body laid out on the floor.

'Look after Mr Livingstone.' Kit Napier's command rang out more curtly than he'd intended, but he could see how shocked the woman was, and this was no time for hysterics. Nursing the fragile old man would give her something to keep her mind off the situation. 'Jake too,' he added as an afterthought.

'Have they cornered her yet?' Kit joined Largo Baines and Major Monaghan at the window overlooking the front of the cabin. They'd taken down the shutters and smashed the single glass pane to provide a firing platform for themselves.

'Doesn't look like it,' replied the major cautiously. 'She disappeared while we were running in and there's no knowing where she is now, but it'll be dark enough in the depths of the barn to make it difficult to locate her. Any case, they're still in there searching for someone. We've put a few shots in to deter them.' He raised his pistol and fired again, but it was too dark to sight with any accuracy and the range was too far for effective shooting, with a handgun anyway.

'Anyone else out there?' Kit called back to the old man, and levered his rifle before taking swift aim. One of the mounted Indians guarding the barn's huge entrance doors slumped forward on his horse, but didn't fall off.

'No.' The answer was made in a short, pain-ridden hiss. 'Just Belinda and those painted devils.'

'They're pulling out.' The sheriff watched the retreating Indians with elation clear in his eyes.

'No,' decided Kit, watching the Indians' progress, 'they're only pulling back out of range. They'll picket the horses under cover and muster to lay siege to us.' He snapped off another couple of shots to encourage the temporary retreat.

'Why doesn't Belinda make a run for it?' Largo Baines had retrieved Mrs Livingstone's rifle and was hurriedly feeding shells into its magazine. 'This is her opportunity while they're still pussy-footing about.'

'I can see a couple of horses being led,' commented Kit, carefully measuring the distances involved. 'Unless Mrs Livingstone shot their riders down, there's at least two Indians on foot, maybe more, probably set on hunting her down in the barn. Be a mighty slow job in the dark if she knows her way about, but it wouldn't be easy for her to cut and run either.' He took stock of the situation one more time. 'Take my rifle, Major. The sheriff's right about one thing; this is her opportunity, maybe the only one she'll get.'

Before anyone could object, Kit slipped, lithe as an eel, through the open window and dropped to the ground, snaking his way into the dubious cover around the side of the cabin. Indian attention was still mainly centred on the outbuildings, but it was only the rapid onset of night that could have hidden his progress from them. Those of his companions who could still stand watched from the window, though they saw no sign of him heading for the barn.

There was a good reason for this; Kit deliberately didn't set out to approach the outbuilding by the most direct route, but began to sneak in a wide circle that would bring him in from an unexpected direction. While some vestige of twilight remained, he sought out cover in the shadowed places; a swift dart to lie flat against the well head; another to slip quietly along the rails of a fence; until eventually he melted into the background of a small copse. From there it was an easy matter to use the folds in the land to approach his target from the rear, quite undetected by the attacking Indians, some of whom were beginning to exchange a desultory fire with the men in the cabin.

A brief cry of exultation went up from their attackers when one of the lesser outbuildings went up in flames, but by the time Kit had made his way into the barn through a badly repaired tear in the fabric, the interior was virtually pitch black and he had to pause to adjust himself to the strange game of hide and seek that was evidently still underway. There were Indian braves assembled inside, three or four so far as he could guess from the sounds that echoed through the darkness. They didn't have to worry about the noise while they were seeking a slip of a girl, and although she'd evidently evaded them so far, they seemed to be gathered in a line to sweep the entire building from one end to the other. No doubt others were posted by the doors to prevent any attempt by their quarry to escape.

Kit drew back, burrowing into the straw, but it appeared they'd already passed his position, and in time a medley of curses showed their plan had failed so far as the girl was concerned as well. Kit quietly reached up and detected the rough beams that held up the loft, apparently forming a mezzanine floor that provided additional storage around all four walls to the barn, leaving the central part open. Whether the Indians knew of the loft he couldn't tell, nor did it matter; they had other methods to smoke out the hiding girl. A spark flashed somewhere in the depths of the barn and shadows began to grow and dance with the flames. They had torched the building. Another cheer sounded outside, and Kit, realizing the game would soon be up, swiftly sprang up into the roof space, heedless of the noise he made. It was here he'd last seen Livingstone's daughter, and he still hoped to find her before the Indians.

One brave had, however, beaten him to the loft, and attracted by the scuffling made when Kit swung crazily upwards, bounded forward to catch the scout unexpectedly from behind. One muscular arm clamped tight around Kit's throat, while the other wielded a wicked blade, with which he attempted to stab his captive.

Kit struggled desperately but, taken unawares, was able to do no more than deflect the thrusting weapon. The Indian set himself to strike again, but was diverted from his purpose by the sudden arrival of the girl, who must have been hidden close by. The angry crackling of the fire lit up the scene in lurid shades of dull, smoky red when she grabbed at his wrist, only to be sent spinning across the loose plank flooring by the full force of a blow from his forearm. Nevertheless, her intervention had provided the scout with time enough to grasp his captor's knife arm, and the two men began a titanic struggle for life.

The Indian still held an advantage in that his arm, locked around Kit's throat, was restricting his breathing, but with a firm grip holding off the knife, the fight began to take place on a more even footing. Kit arched his body and writhed, bucking and whirling to throw his attacker off his back, all the time twisting the greasy, copper-hued wrist in his grasp.

A wicked, back-angled thrust of his elbow ploughed into the Indian's ribs and the iron grip on the scout's throat loosened for the merest moment. A brief respite only, but enough to give the white man his second wind; a supple twist of the body, a jerk across his back and the savage knifeman was thrown over his shoulders. The Indian may no longer have been in charge, but he reacted as quickly as ever, rolling lithely to his feet and attempting a savage slash that would have disembowelled the scout if he hadn't leapt back lightly, fumbling for his gun.

The red man dropped under the clubbing action of a Winchester repeating rifle before he had time to draw, and Kit was left looking into the eyes of a tall, thickset man; undoubtedly of Indian cast, but wearing clothes more suited to a white man.

'Come.' The newcomer was evidently a man of few words, but he suited his actions to his speech, and grasping the dazed girl by one arm, thrust her between the two of them before he began to advance towards the worst of the fire at the front of the barn.

Kit held back, motioning towards the darker side walls where he'd made his entrance, but their new companion demurred. 'They'll be waiting for us outside; through the flames is the only way to escape. Your friends will provide covering fire once we're out of here.'

It made sense, but the flames were high and the heat intense. Then with an almighty crash the huge doors at the front of the barn collapsed creating a temporary thinning of the conflagration at that point. With a triumphant yell, the three companions leapt from the upper reaches of the barn and burst through the opening.

At first it seemed they'd taken their foes completely by surprise, but by the time they'd reached the cabin they were coming under heavy fire again, and it was only the uncertain light of the flickering fire that merged the dancing shadows with their own fast moving sprint that saved them. The door opened briefly while they tumbled in.

'Who the devil's this?' Jake Lassiter might have been flat out on the floor, but he had a gun in his hand and he trained it steadily on their Indian companion.

CHAPTER 6

SIEGE

'Never mind that now, Jake.' Kit took charge of the situation at once, his eyes flickering around the defences already in place. 'He's on our side, at the least.' He measured the thick, weathered logs that made up the cabin and found they passed muster. Even if the Indians could get close enough to fire them, and that was a big if considering the cabin had been built with defence in mind, it'd take a while to burn through, unlike the flimsy outbuildings. 'What's up in the roof?'

'I sleep on the platform up there.' Belinda had hunkered down next to her father, nervously smoothing the sweat off his forehead. 'The roof-light above leads out on to a flat roof, but it's probably shuttered up.'

'Will you take the roof, Sheriff?' Though politely couched as a question, there was no doubt the scout had taken charge and expected to be obeyed. 'All the outbuildings that overlook the place are burning so you'll be safe enough on top so long as you keep your head down. If we can prevent them savages creeping up behind us, the siege is half won. I'll send someone up to help you.'

'Major.' He turned to the ex-army officer, who still stood guard by the window. 'You're in charge of defences on the ground floor.' He pulled aside a curtain guarding one side of the room and exposed the Livingstones' bed, nodding his head in a satisfied manner when he realized there were no more entrances to police.

'How's Mr Livingstone doing?'

'He's feverish,' returned Tallulah shortly. 'Don't rely on him for any help.'

'What's she doing here?' Kit had been aware of some interplay between the two women and Belinda's harsh question confirmed there was trouble in the making if he didn't nip it in the bud.

'Trying to stay alive, the same as the rest of us,' he told the girl shortly, and gave her a job to keep her mind active. 'Belinda, you're in charge of food and water from now on. Take an inventory, especially drinking water, and ration it appropriately. You'd better assume we'll be cut off for a week at least.'

'What about my father?'

'You can nurse him between jobs. Tallulah will help you with the cooking and look after Jake and any other casualties.' He softened his attitude a mite. 'I'm sorry about your mother.'

'Thank you, but there's no need to worry about

me,' Belinda rose with fresh determination apparent in her manner, and began to take stock of supplies. 'I'll work now and grieve later. There's no point in a crying fit while those savages are still waiting outside.'

'I haven't had time to thank you yet.' Kit turned to the tall, silent figure of the Indian who'd aided him in the barn and thrust out his hand. The return handshake was firm without being too strong.

'No need for your thanks; I'm in as much trouble as you are.'

'You say you're in trouble, but just who are you?' Jake broke in on them again, still troubled at the stranger's sudden arrival and Indian-like appearance.

'My name's David,' the stranger began in an educated voice, 'and I farm a smallholding west of here. I used to be welcome at the lodges, but I'm half-breed. With the war against the white man flaring up, I'm no longer trusted by my own people.'

'What were you doing in the barn?' The old driver wasn't mollified by the half-breed's glib answers.

'Hiding. I've been hunted down for several days, and now the war has started, I'm fair game for any Indian.'

'It's your fault we were attacked!' Belinda accused. 'They were chasing you.'

'No.' He refuted the suggestion immediately. 'The warriors outside wear paint. They're here to make war, not chase a stray half-breed. They couldn't have known I'd be here, in any case.'

'You're mighty sure of that?' Kit asked the question.

58

'My father was once a mighty warrior, high in the councils of the lodge. He taught me much before he died; how to track and also how to hide.' Simple pride in his own ability shone through. 'These warriors are but dogs beneath his feet.'

'Guess you'll do,' admitted Jake. 'Getting shot up must have curdled my brain. If you helped Kit out then you're OK.'

'You'd better deploy yourself up on the roof,' decided Kit. 'We need every man we can get up there if we're not going to be over-run. The window's all very well, but it only covers the front of the cabin.' He considered their placements a moment longer. 'Tell the sheriff to get some sleep, but not to leave his post. He's been travelling a long time and deserves a spell of rest.'

David nodded gravely and began to ascend the makeshift ladder.

'I'd better go up, too.' Jake began to lever himself off the floor, wincing when the pain hit him.

'You'll get some sleep,' commanded the scout. 'We'll need you at the window when they attack.'

'When will that be?'

'A couple of hours, I'd guess. Be sheer suicide to press home an attack before the flames die down; they'd be sitting ducks lit up by the fire.' He turned to the taciturn figure at the window. 'You'd better get some sleep too, Major. I'll stand first watch.'

Kit took his place by the window, hanging back behind the heavy jambs for the sake of concealment, and watched the barn begin to collapse while the flames flung their gaseous fumes high into the evening sky. He could still see figures in the background, the fire glinting off their copper skin and hideously painted faces, but they took care to remain well out of effective range. A gentle scent wafted around him and he realized the Livingstone girl had joined him.

'How's your father now?' He asked the question gently, more aware than ever of how fragile she seemed.

'He's sleeping.' Belinda's answer was short, made without embellishment. Tears formed in her eyes, but she was too proud to let them drop. 'He won't survive; wouldn't have lived much longer in any case.'

Kit looked at her and she explained.

'He was a teacher back East until he contracted tuberculosis. The doctors advised him to move out West where the climate would suit him better. It almost killed Mother; she was born into a well-off Boston family and hated it out here. She only came to keep Pa alive, and she always told me we'd go straight back home when it happened.' She strangled a stricken sob. 'And now she's died out here in the wilderness, just as she always feared.'

'Do you enjoy it out here?'

'I was less than two years old when we travelled West and I loved my father too much to want anything else. Besides this was my home, the only life I ever knew. I was too young to remember what living was like back East and I'm promised to one of the sheriff's deputies in Goldrush, so I guess I never will. It's a hard life to my mother's way of thinking, but I'm used to living like that and wouldn't have it any other way.' She reached out and caught hold of Kit's arm for comfort, dropping her head while she began to reminisce.

'You'd better sleep now.' Kit broke the developing silence before it became too demanding. 'Seems like everyone else is.'

The first signs of an impending assault developed around midnight. The fires had burned low, leaving no more than a glow where the buildings had once stood. There was nothing to see in the pitch black beyond, but Kit fancied he heard the sound of pattering feet when some careless brave, too young or too confident to heed, took up his position. A low murmur from far beyond the yard confirmed his suspicions and he poked the major into wakefulness.

'Take the window,' he commanded. 'Jake will cover it with you.' The wounded driver, who'd instantly roused himself from his blankets was already stumbling stiffly into position.

Kit climbed silently on to the roof to find the two men stationed up there awake and staring alertly into the gloom. He looked around to find the situation defended by a low palisade of logs, part of the original defences when the cabin was built.

'This fellow reckons they're coming,' grumbled the sheriff, 'but I can't see a thing.'

'He's right, Sheriff, they're massing to attack. Our

job is to stop them getting close enough to do any damage. Should be an easy matter to accomplish, there's no cover within thirty yards of the cabin. Watch the stockade; there's enough cover down there to hide an army in this light. They'll make a rush at us, but we'll be ready for them.'

He turned to David, who was watching the rear of the property. 'Any sign?'

'Ten, maybe twelve. On the edge of those trees.'

Kit peered over towards the very copse he'd used to disguise his own approach to the barn so short a time before. There was a picket fence there too, closer to the cabin and the well head. That's where they'd be making for.

'They'll rush us from the well,' he told David, who nodded sagely and patted his rifle.

'Used this a time or two in the last few days,' he told the scout, 'it won't let me down.'

The assault happened too suddenly for anyone to determine exactly where the first shots came from. All of a sudden the air was full of wild war whoops and the thunder of guns. The beleaguered party immediately hit back with their own weapons, pouring out a murderous fire aimed at the flashes from the Indian's own guns.

A copper face, slashed with streaks of blue, red and yellow, appeared on the edge of the roof and Kit shot it at point-blank range. A guttural command and the Indians withdrew in good order, slipping noiselessly back into their hiding places to await the next assault.

The scout grinned at his companions. 'We've made it too hot for them,' he confirmed, then slipped through the roof-light to check for casualties down below. But before he could ask the question another batch of firing broke out in the night.

'What the devil?' Kit hauled himself back on to the roof with a curse and stared out into the night.

'Horse soldiers.' David supplied the answer and Kit's own eyes confirmed the suspicion when two horsemen galloped flat out into the yard, throwing their horses on to their haunches when they drew to an abrupt halt.

'Alleluia,' cried the sheriff exultantly when he took in their uniforms. 'We're saved.'

'Let them in,' Kit screamed through the roof-light and took a fresh grip on his rifle.

Several mounted warriors arrived in the wake of the soldiers and began their assault immediately, but with Jake and the major laying down a steady fire from the window and all three riflemen on the roof in support, those who didn't drop swiftly retired.

Kit, satisfied that David was still listening for any sign of further attack, made his way below to greet the new arrivals.

'Why Major, didn't expect to see more army here.' The speaker was wearing sergeant's stripes, but spoke with an air of confidence unusual in a non-commissioned man speaking to a high ranking officer. 'Did your detachment get wiped out, too?'

'No, Sergeant. I was on the stage.' The major peered over the burly sergeant's shoulder at the man behind. 'Lieutenant?' His voice sounded surprised that it hadn't been the officer who took the lead and reported to him first.

'Sir.' The youngster sounded diffident in the extreme, and Kit had no doubt the sergeant had completely dominated him in whatever mission they were on.

Not that it would be difficult. The sergeant was a bull of a man, barely able to contain his muscular form in the stained uniform he wore, while the lieutenant was painfully small, short and skinny, and almost too young for his commission. With the newcomers' attention still fixed on the major, Kit found time to examine the youngster's holstered gun, slung low on his hip in a manner more reminiscent of a gunman than an officer in the United States Army.

'What happened?' The major spoke quietly to calm the youngster's fears, but Kit noticed he didn't tell them his own days in the army were over.

'Work detail, sir.' The sergeant answered for his officer, but hesitated long enough before uttering the last word to make it sound like a studied insult. 'We were caught out in the open and didn't stand a chance. A few of us got away and rode like the wind.'

'I believe the lieutenant can speak for himself, Sergeant.' The major fumed quietly, but there was no point in quarrelling in view of their current perilous situation, and neither did he any longer have the authority to discipline the sergeant as he deserved.

'It's as the sergeant says, sir.' The boy had pulled

himself together, but he still looked bemused at landing himself in front of a senior officer. 'What do we do now?'

'Kit Napier's in charge here.' The major pointed out the scout. 'He'll see to your dispositions.'

'Elmore Bunting.' The sergeant introduced himself at once, holding out one huge paw that totally engulfed Kit's own hand. His grip was firm, and the scout felt the strength behind it. 'The kid. . . .' His voice dropped off a notch while he corrected himself. 'The lieutenant's name is Jacobs; Nat Jacobs, if he doesn't mind me making free of it. He's a bit of a sharp-shooter; give him a position up on the roof and he'll soon cut them savages down to size.' He rubbed his belly ostentatiously. 'Have you got any food? We ain't eaten in a while.'

CHAPTER 7

RAISING THE ODDS

With the beleagured party hourly expecting a further assault on their position, the rest of the night passed uncomfortably. The unexpected increase in their combined firepower enabled Kit to stagger the watches more easily, but since nobody believed their enemies had finished for the night, none of them could find solace in sleep for more than a few minutes at a time.

Once he'd realized the party were going to get no further rest the scout called the party together to decide on their next move. It wasn't yet dawn and David and Tallulah volunteered to keep watch on the roof while the remainder discussed their options.

'Why haven't they attacked us again?' The major was the first to voice the question on everyone's lips.

'I guess we're in a strong position.' Kit shrugged his shoulders. The trite answer sounded lame to his own ears; there must have been a couple of dozen braves out there, even allowing for any losses during the night attack. 'This cabin's well placed to repel a frontal attack and we've already forced a stand-off,' he went on. 'Maybe the Indians believe they can starve us into submission; if so, they could wait until we're too weak to defend ourselves. There're not to know we're provisioned to survive a long siege.'

The young lieutenant cleared his throat bashfully, but subsided into blushing silence when his audience turned to look at him.

'What the lieutenant means,' the sergeant broke in, before his officer could speak, 'is that we were ambushed by a much bigger war party. They took out most of the troop before we managed to escape. We left them looting the dead men, but they can't be far behind.'

'Then they're waiting for reinforcements, perhaps their chief, too,' Kit decided. 'How many were there?'

'Fifty or sixty of the devils,' decided the sergeant. 'Wearing paint; too many for us to stand against with less than a dozen fighting men. We were gathering wood and they cut down most of the lads before we reached our guns.'

'How come you managed to escape?' There was a tinge of derision in Major Monaghan's voice.

'Guess we were just lucky, Major.' The sergeant flushed angrily, but the major didn't push the point any further.

Just as well, thought Kit, we're in enough trouble without fighting amongst ourselves.

'We can't hold off a war party that size,' he went on to declare, his face showing none of his private misgivings. 'One of us has to give these Indians the slip and make his way to the fort at Goldrush.'

'That person has to be you, Kit.' The major's opinion of the scout's current abilities had changed since the attack on the stagecoach. 'You're the only one of us with any chance of bringing it off.'

'David might be a better choice; he'd blend in with our attackers more easily and by his own admission he's successfully evaded them for several days already. Getting out's going to be the first test; they'll have set a guard it won't be easy to get past.'

'No.' The major was emphatic on that point, backed up by a general murmur of opinion. 'He might be able to do it, but why should he bother with us once he'd escaped? And even if he did, why should the commander at the fort believe his story?'

'I'd be suspicious myself if an Indian turned up when I was in charge,' declared the sheriff belligerently, 'especially if there's a general uprising in the offing. No sense in taking chances with people's lives and leading a patrol into danger on the word of an unknown savage.'

'OK,' Kit acknowledged the decision. 'I'll have to sneak out before first light to stand any chance of escaping. I guess you're in charge now, Major.' He stared out into the night where the eastern peaks were already beginning to show in a line against the coming dawn, 'but don't expect relief to come too soon, the fort's a long way off for a man on foot.'

'There's a horse corralled up the draw,' Belinda offered unexpectedly. 'Two or three miles north-east of the farm, by an old line hut. I spent the last couple of days up there myself and left it tethered since I only planned to stay home for a few hours to collect some tools. This war party must have approached from the other direction and they've been kept pretty busy ever since; they might not have discovered it yet.'

'Thanks, that's worth checking out,' Kit acknowledged.

'I'll put some provisions together for you,' the girl told him helpfully.

'Get back as soon as you can.' The major took Kit aside before he left on his mission. 'I don't like the look of our guests from the army detachment. The sergeant's too free with his manners for my liking and the lad is no officer; his uniform is a disgrace and he's wearing that gun like he knows how to use it. The sergeant's uniform doesn't fit either, come to that, and it's showing a bloody hole where he's got no wounds.'

'What are you suggesting?'

'I don't know,' admitted the major shrugging his shoulders. 'I just don't believe they're army. Apart from their general demeanour, I've never seen either of them before, despite the fort at Goldrush being the only army post in the neighbourhood. Something's wrong about them, but I can't put my finger on it. I know one thing, however: they'd leave us in the lurch without a qualm if it suited them.'

'You'll need all the guns you can get to defend this place against a party as big as the one they're describing,' advised the scout. 'I don't trust them either, but it's hard to see what harm they could do you; or would even want to while they're holed up here! After all,' he concluded, 'they need you as much as you need them.' He stuck out his hand. 'Good luck, Major.'

Kit left the building via the roof; slipping quietly over the western wall and lowering himself gently until he hung at arm's length before dropping noiselessly into the deeper patches of darkness left by dawn's breaking light. Silently he scooted down the shadows towards the corral he'd already noted, hoping the broken shards of light and shade flung by the rough fencing while the dawn light grew rapidly stronger would hide his progress. He didn't try to kid himself he'd escaped undetected; their attackers must have pickets out awaiting just such a move, but at least none of them had taken a shot at him yet.

A wide-leafed bush loomed up and, drawing his knife, he crept into its dark shadows to await events. If anyone had detected his escape they'd be on his tail and the blade would be his silent friend where a shot from his revolver could only draw in the remainder of their enemies. A single brave would represent good odds to him; the Indian would have to decide he was truly a foe before attacking, whereas anyone outside the cabin had to be Kit's enemy and he need have no qualms in killing them.

In the event, it seemed he had escaped unseen after all, for after several minutes listening to nothing more sinister than the scurrying of an inquisitive rodent, Kit decided no one was hunting him. Accordingly he slunk away from the farm, circling wide around the area he suspected the Indians had made their encampment, but always heading north and east to locate the corral Belinda had told him of. The eerie silence might have unnerved a lesser man, but he matched it with his own stealthy movements.

Progress was necessarily slow for a man who wanted to keep away from any marked trail, and by the time he'd located the line hut the sun had been up a couple of hours. A brief scan of the environs showed the corral with the promised horse still in occupation, but three paint ponies were drawn up outside the old shack, which was evidently being looted while he watched.

With the safety of his companions depending on a swift return with help, Kit had no time to think of the consequences. No sooner had his questing eyes located an open fronted lean-to that contained a saddle, than he was out in the open, loping silently towards its maw. Reins and bit was all he needed to control the horse and he took them at a run; all too aware the Indian ponies were becoming too skittish not to draw their owners out. He raced towards the corral, no longer caring how much noise he made, and leapt on the waiting horse's back. A hasty kick took out one fence pole and he spurred the animal on as the Indians surged out of the hut. A flurry of shots had them diving for cover, but he knew they'd soon be on his trail and high-tailed it for the route that offered most cover.

A convenient bend in the trail offered him the opportunity he sought, and he recklessly ploughed through the thick brush towards the shelter of a band of trees. He wasn't used to riding bareback without a rein and vented a sigh of relief when he was able to slide off the animal's back under the concealment of low lying branches. He used the respite to slide on the bit and reins, gently stroking the horse's muzzle to keep it calm, while out on the trail three braves passed in a shower of dust and war whoops.

Kit knew better than to remain in hiding. The braves were young and in their precipitate haste had failed to observe the swathe he'd cut through the outlying brush. They'd realize their mistake and retrace their steps all too soon. Instead he pushed on through the trees, leading his horse until the vegetation thinned and he could safely ride again.

The young warriors had less respect for their own mounts and the scout was soon aware of riders plunging through the thick brush to his rear. In full daylight, in such dense undergrowth there was no way he could hide his tracks from anyone other than the merest tyro and he didn't attempt the task. The ground was rising to his left and he took that direction hoping he'd reach easier going on the higher ground. He knew when the chasing savages reached his point of deviation for he heard them whoop in triumph.

The woodland ended suddenly on the edge of a chasm, and far below he could hear the splashing of a young stream. He measured the distance across the yawning gap and realized he couldn't have made the jump even if his horse had space in which to work up to a gallop. He dragged the animal along the rocky edge, carefully inspecting the drop at his feet. He might scramble down himself, but not with his mount, which would then effectively give away his own position. Cursing under his breath he began to edge higher up the narrow canyon, staying back in the cover of the tree-line, and trying to measure the approach of his enemies from their excited chatter.

He was perhaps 200 yards above them when they broke through the tree-line and on to the edge of the chasm, more or less where he himself had stood so short a time before. He drew back and watched from the shelter of a bush. With no bruised undergrowth to betray his movements it was several minutes before the braves made their decision. They scouted both up and down the canyon edge before deciding correctly.

Kit took out his pistol and waited patiently for them to approach him, leading their horses, clearly unaware he was so close at hand. He stepped into the open to fire for maximum accuracy. It was long range for a handgun. But the shot struck home and one of the young Indian braves shrieked as he fell, then shrieked again when he lost his footing and went over the edge. A long, drawn-out howl stopped with shocking abruptness when the dull echo of his body's impact rang out of the chasm far below them.

Kit rode. He leapt on the horse and urged it to a reckless gallop down through the forest. The other two Indians had disappeared, but this was no time for congratulation, or for sparing his horse. A bough appeared in his path and he flattened himself against his mount's out-thrust neck just in time to avoid being hurled from its back. A continuous spray of twigs and leaves lashed his face, drawing blood, but still he rode on, kicking the animal into even greater speed. In the back of his mind he could hear the thunder of his pursuers, blood crazed and eager to avenge their erstwhile companion.

Eventually he edged his sweating mount back towards the trail. The terrain would be more open, but so too would the risk of injury be reduced. He swung on to the dusty path that led down towards the plains and Goldrush at a gallop, throwing a glance over his shoulder now and then. One Indian pony burst out of the forest on his heels, but the where-abouts of the other remained a mystery.

One minute passed, then two, with both pursued and pursuer at full stretch, then Kit decided to take a chance. If he held on to his present course he might outrun the Indian, but would be left with an exhausted mount, delaying his return to Goldrush. He swung the horse around in its own length and charged the on-coming brave.

It was a bold move that took the young warrior by

surprise. Kit shot twice from the hip, but so far as he could tell failed to hit his target. Not surprising considering the swaying speed of both animals. They met in a flash; Kit lashing out with his pistol while the Indian made an awkward thrust with his tomahawk. The scout turned his mount again, but the fight was over. His barrel had made contact with the young brave's head and the Indian had fallen.

Kit stopped his horse over the other's prone body and decided there was nothing more to fear. Shooting the fellow would only alert the remaining Indian still somewhere out in the forest. Gathering the reins he clapped his boots hard against the animal's haunches and urged it forward at a gallop. He'd have to circle around to cut a trail for Goldrush, but with the animal between his legs still relatively fresh, he had no doubt he'd make it before the day was out.

CHAPTER 8

PALE WOLF
SHOWS HIS HAND

In fact Kit had travelled barely a mile before he came
across a sight that astounded him. He'd thrust high
on to a rocky plateau that offered few chances to any
follower of effectively tracking him, and riding close
to the escarpment, looked down on a wide, grassy
plain. The half-breed, David, and the girl from the
saloon were riding in tandem; not galloping, but
nevertheless in an obvious hurry. Had they escaped
the siege too? David might have the skill to evade
their savage enemies, but Kit doubted whether he
could have done it with the girl in tow. It seemed
more likely they were fleeing from a successful
assault, having escaped in the confusion of a mêlée.
If so, the siege was over and his own task superfluous.

The scout stifled his initial temptation to fire into
the air to attract their attention while he tracked

their progress with rapidly mounting trepidation. It quickly became obvious that Tallulah's horse was being led and he had an increasing suspicion the girl's hands were pinioned. David had shown no sign of attraction to the woman, but if he'd abducted her, there had to be some reason behind the act. Kit urged his horse towards the edge of the escarpment and nudged it down the steep slopes to the plain below. He'd follow in their tracks and come up on the pair at a place of his own choosing.

Easier said than done; an hour's hard riding and the tracks ended abruptly at the entrance to a rock-strewn canyon which soon divided into a dozen loosely connected draws, any one of which the pair could have taken. Kit sighed heavily, and spurred his tiring horse up the steepest trail, seeking the higher ground which might give him a wider view of his quarry. It didn't, and the dispirited scout was driven into riding a search pattern in the hopes of cutting their trail. It was slow and patient work that almost failed to deliver.

It was on one of his wider castings that he sighted the encampment. Indians! By the half-breed's own admission he'd not be welcome at the camp-fires and the scout would have drawn back until his eyes picked up a swirl of scarlet. It was the girl's dress, burning bright against the dull backdrop of the Indian camp.

The scout dismounted and having secured his horse, crept forward to reconnoitre the scene. Tallulah was secured to a tall wooden stake, her hands drawn high on its rough hewn length, and her dress torn down to her waist. Even at a distance Kit's sharp eyes could see she'd been whipped and was still being tormented by two young Indian women who were poking her with what looked like sharpened sticks. His keen eyes searched the village dispassionately, but he could detect no sign of Indian braves and took a chance that only their squaws were actually in residence.

The two Indian women taunting and stabbing at the white girl ran lithely for the cover of the surrounding brush when he galloped towards the camp roaring out a terrifying battle whoop. Ignoring both them and the old crone who was squatting on the ground outside a nearby tepee engaged in mending a leather vest, Kit slid off his horse and ran to Tallulah's side. His pistol was at the ready, but as soon as he realized they had the camp to themselves, he holstered it and drew his knife, quickly slicing through the rawhide strips that secured the girl to the stake.

'Hurry,' he told her urgently, 'we'd better get out of here before someone raises the alarm.' The girl was dividing her attention between an attempt to cover her breasts with the remnants of her torn bodice and in rubbing life back into her bruised and abraded wrists. Kit made a dart towards the old crone, who eventually acknowledged his presence by scuttling into the tepee behind her, but it hadn't been the old woman he was after. Deftly he picked up the discarded vest and threw it to the girl while he remounted. Tallulah drew on the Indian garment, dropping her attempt at modesty in her haste to don the garment, and wincing when it stretched across the marks of the lash that decorated her back.

Taking his proffered hand, she scrambled awkwardly on to the horse behind him and hung on to his waist while they set off with a lurch that almost left her unseated again.

At first their flight was pure adrenalin, taken at a gallop, until at length the scout began to throttle back, realizing they couldn't continue to run at that pace for long. Nevertheless, with the ever present threat of pursuit in the forefront of his mind, he kept the overloaded horse moving at a trot.

'What happened to you?' His questioning voice sounded harsh after the silence he'd maintained during the initial phase of their escape.

'The half-breed,' replied Tallulah, gasping audibly as the heavy leather vest chafed her wounds whenever the horse missed a step on the uneven ground. 'His name amongst the Indians is Pale Wolf.'

'The renegade who's been dealing with the saloon keeper for arms?'

'Correct. From what he told me, he rose to prominence amongst the tribesmen, especially the bolder young braves, by promising them guns in return for gold. It didn't make him popular with the local chiefs, and when they discovered Jem was planning a double cross they pinned the blame on Pale Wolf. He and his followers were hunted down, but somehow he got to hear about Jem Horne's murder and my flight from Goldrush. He might not have met her, but he knew Jem's partner was a woman and attacked the stagecoach under the impression I was escaping with the loot. After we escaped, he must have tracked us as far as the Livingstone ranch and, finding it under attack, took his chance to infiltrate the cabin.'

'Are you saying he killed his own man to save my life?' Kit was incredulous at the Indian chief's duplicity.

'No, I don't think so. Not exactly, anyway. From what I understood, the ranch was already under attack by another faction.' She fell silent a moment before adding a singular rider, 'One who may have had better information about the double cross than Pale Wolf.'

'When did he abduct you? What about the others? Didn't they try to stop him?' Kit had more questions to throw at the girl.

'We were still up on the roof when you left. Pale Wolf and I were on watch and the sheriff climbed up to join us. Must have been about an hour after you disappeared that Pale Wolf grabbed me from behind. He stuck a gag in my mouth before I realized what was happening and tied my wrists.' Kit felt her body shudder behind him and her heavy breasts crushed harder against his back. 'I think the sheriff was dead,' she went on in a tremulous voice. 'He was lying very still and there was a lot of blood. Not that I had much time to take it in. Pale Wolf didn't explain himself, just dropped me over the edge of the roof and tossed me over his shoulder once he'd leapt down himself.'

'What about the Indians?'

'I don't think there were any; they didn't bother us, at any rate. Pale Wolf carried me about half a mile to where he had horses waiting. Once mounted I was led to his camp and tethered to the stake for questioning.'

'How come he left you there?'

'I talked,' she admitted. 'I let him whip me until I couldn't stand the pain and then confessed. Told him the gold was hidden under the seats on the stagecoach.'

'Is it?'

'Not that I know of, but then I never was Jem's partner. Not in this enterprise or any other.'

'Did he believe you?'

'I think so. That's why I didn't speak straight away. I was scared he wouldn't if I spoke too soon.' She shuddered and hung on tight to the scout as though her memories were scarred by the whipping she'd received.

'He'd have found out you were lying soon enough.'

Tallulah shuddered again. 'Don't remind me. I always knew it was only a temporary reprieve. I expected him to move on to more painful methods of extracting information when he came back, but I didn't have much to tell him.'

'What about the other band? Those attacking the Livingstone Ranch.'

'Chief War Bonnet. I heard him cursing their intervention.'

'You said they may have better information?'

'Belinda. I'm not saying she was Jem's accomplice in selling guns to the Indians, but she was his lover.'

Kit was so surprised he stopped the horse and stared over his shoulder at the girl. 'Are you sure? I can't see a girl like her having anything to do with Jem Horne. How'd they meet anyway?'

'I don't know how, or where, he met her,' Tallulah replied, 'but I caught her sneaking in or out of Jem's quarters above the saloon on more than one occasion. Don't be fooled by her butter-wouldn't-melt-in-my-mouth airs; even nice girls can fall in love and Jem Horne's an accomplished flirt. I should know, that's how I ended up in this mess. Besides, when you're regularly sneaking out of a man's apartment in the early hours there's only one conclusion to be drawn.'

'I still can't believe a girl like Belinda was involved in gun running,' Kit told her eventually. 'The lives of her own family would have been on the line, if nothing else.' He spurred the horse on again, still attempting to make sense of this new, and potentially damning, information. 'Why didn't you tell Pale Wolf about her? It might have got you off the hook.'

'I was dead meat the moment he kidnapped me,' she replied. 'If I'd told him that story, he wouldn't have believed it any more than you did. He'd have tortured me until there were no doubts left in his mind, and once I'd served my purpose, handed me over to the women. Those two back in the camp were already poised to go to work; they were poking me with sharpened sticks when you arrived. As soon as he gave the word they'd have used their knives on me; cut me up for fun until I eventually died in agony. The more time I could buy myself, the better.'

Kit grunted and nudged the horse's face towards the steeper hills. For several minutes they climbed steadily up a steep-sided canyon in silence, until, with a hiss of satisfaction, the scout found the landmark he'd been looking for.

'Wait here,' he commanded when he dismounted, and vanished behind a shimmer of vegetation that seemed to grow out of the bare rock face.

Time passed and Tallulah nervously peered back down the canyon, expecting at any moment to find the Indian chief had tracked them down. Her apprehensions grew as the minutes stretched, so much so that when Kit reappeared she jumped in alarm. Tactfully ignoring her fears, he took the reins and, beckoning her to follow, led the horse into the midst of a jumble of thorn bushes which clutched at her clothes and skin with all the impatience of a demon lover. The faint trail, only visible once its leafy border had been breached, led steeply up though a narrow side canyon, barely more than a split in the rock, but evidently damp enough to feed the skeins of moss and ferns that hung around its walls in abundance. A few minutes tough climb over an uneven bed of rock saw them enter a magical bower, a bowl-shaped enclosure in the rocky fastness with a pool at its centre fed from a small waterfall that burst from the cliffs above.

'Aren't we going back to warn the others?' Tallulah stared around the bower in surprise.

'Not with Pale Wolf and a parcel of braves on the loose. Once they discover your escape, we'll have the devils right on our tail. We're riding two up on a tired animal and they'd quickly run us down.'

'Won't they be able to track us here?'

'The trail we rode is too rocky to make tracking us a simple matter and Pale Wolf won't have time to cast about. I fancy he'll make an educated guess that we'll be riding towards the Livingstone ranch, if only to warn our companions. Well, they'll have to run their own risks; we'll travel by night, daylight's much too chancy for my liking.'

'You already knew this place existed, didn't you? It wasn't chance that took us to it.'

'I've known about it for years. It's always useful to know of a good source of water in this sort of country.'

'Who else knows about it?' Tallulah cast a worried glance at the way up from the trail.

'Indians, I guess. I've camped out here on several occasions, but never seen anyone else. There's been sign though; I'm not the only man to use it.'

'Pale Wolf?'

'Could be, but he's been back East from what you say. We're safe enough for the moment. Now, get that top off and I'll clean up your back.' Kit stared at the girl, as though seeing her for the first time. The leather vest was made for a man and laced over at the front, leaving Tallulah's breasts half naked. He felt the inevitable reaction and turned away to save her blushes.

Tallulah felt her face flaring. She'd seen just where his eyes had rested and cursed herself for her embarrassment. Damn it, she told herself, he's not the first man to stare at your breasts. Turning away, she began to unlace the vest and draw it off her shoulders, wincing when the dried blood stuck it to her body. Bare to the waist, she sank down beside the pool and waited, her arms protectively wrapped around her chest.

Kit sank to his haunches behind her and began to bathe the bloody weals. He could see from the crisscrossed bruises just how many strokes the Indian chief had laid on, but the skin had only been punctured in a few places and, to his relief, the cuts were clean. The women with the sharpened sticks had caused further minor abrasions under her ribs, and he went to clean them up.

'No need, I'll do that,' Tallulah told him. 'I need a bath after all I've been through.' In an abrupt turn around from her previous assumption of modesty she stood up and allowed her arms to drop away from her body. 'Is it safe?'

He nodded. 'The horse will warn us if anyone creeps up.' His eyes ran over her naked torso appreciatively.

She turned to face him directly, offering the view he wanted; her breasts, plump and firm, with rosy nipples standing proud on a pink background. Unashamed at his direct stare, she wrinkled her nose in distaste. 'You need a bath too.'

Kit knew that much was true; he hadn't washed for days, not since he'd gone off on the bender that landed him in jail. He swallowed hard when the saloon girl began to push down her skirts, her breasts swaying while she bent from the waist to ease them off her feet. Her boots and stockings went next, and finally the pretty bloomers, pale pink dressed with showers of lace. Abruptly she leaned forward and kissed him on the mouth.

'What was that for?'

'For saving me.' Tallulah began to wade into the water, her hips swaying gently to an erotic tune that drew the scout's eyes irrevocably to the play in her taut buttocks. He knew they'd soon be making love and impatiently began to strip.

Once in the water they began to play, throwing water at each other in a gay abandon that was totally foreign to the desperate situation they were facing. Their bodies collided and Tallulah kissed him again, skipping out of his reach when he tried to trap her in his arms. Another spray of water caused him to lose his footing on the uneven bottom and he disappeared under the surface, only to reappear in a welter of foam. She came to him then, rubbing him down, rinsing off the dirt and sweat with her hands, teasing him with whisper soft caresses while she cleaned his body.

At last she was satisfied with his cleanliness and Kit reached out to grasp her, gasping when she reciprocated his need, pressing her body hard against his own. Oblivious to the danger around them they played in the shallows, coupling hard, then teasing until they coupled again.

Afterwards they lay in the sun, drying themselves while they talked.

'How come you knew about this place?' Tallulah asked the question warily. In her line of work she'd met a lot of men who didn't want to speak of their past, and some of them resorted to violence without warning. She didn't want to think the scout was one of these, but a girl never knew.

'I was brought up in these hills.' Kit surprised her with his candid admission. 'Pa was brought up a mountain man; not here, but before we came West. He married Ma and thought to settle down, but she died soon after I was born. God knows how he managed it with a baby to look after, but he travelled out West and brought me up in the mountains just like his folk before him.

'He taught me wilderness ways: how to trail; how to hunt; how to shoot; and how to live off the country. This is about as far south as we ever came and this dell is just one of the places he showed me; knowing where water can be found in country like this can save your life. Taught me to read and write too. I don't know where he got his learning, but he told me it was as important as feeding myself.'

'What about the Indians?'

'They were our friends in those days. We had a cabin ten, twelve days north of here, but close enough to one of their encampments to trade when Pa thought it expedient. We traded with the settlers too, though I saw more of the redskins than my own race in those days.' Kit paused, his expression closed. 'They came for us one night, a dozen or more braves with paint on their faces. Pa was their friend; how could they do that?'

'What happened?' Tallulah laid a sympathetic hand on his arm, listening with unaffected fascination to his story.

'Pa sent me out to hide in the bushes nearby while he tried to calm them down.' He paused before adding bitterly, 'They took him. The bastards took him, and I could do nothing.' The scout continued his story flatly, his eyes staring into the distance as though he could still see the fight. 'He wasn't armed, never was unless for hunting, but he was a powerful man and he fought them until the end. It came when one of them clubbed him with a tomahawk.

'They carried him away, back to their encampment, and lit the slow fires. I heard him screaming while I shivered with fright, but I was too scared to help. Not that there was anything I could do against such a large party.' Kit stared at the girl from the saloon with tears in his eyes. 'He was strong. It took him a long time to die and next morning, after they'd left, I saw what they'd done to him. I was little more than a boy, but I turned into a man that day. I buried him, and set out on the revenge trail. He'd taught me good, I could trail and fight better than any Indian, and I wasn't too particular how I killed them. It couldn't last though, and I guess I'd have died at their hands eventually if I hadn't found out about the army.

'There were a lot of settlers moving in on the traditional hunting grounds and the local tribes were becoming restless. A few of the bolder spirits amongst them initiated fierce raids on the scattered ranches and the army moved in. I signed on as a scout, still thirsting for revenge, and got it. A few pitched battles saw off any real threat from the Indian braves, but orders were out to finish them for good. At length even my vengeful spirit became jaded by all the bloodshed. We'd ride in and massacre whole villages; men, women and children, anything that moved. By the time we were finished, so was the redskin.

'I'd had my fill of revenge by then, and drifted south. There were still Indians about in this country, hence the army post at Goldrush, but they were peaceable until Pale Wolf showed up. Guess they never needed to worry about the white man taking their land around here, conditions are too arid for wholesale ranching or farming; just a few isolated folks like the Livingstones. I got a job as guard on the stage and took to drink. Sometimes it helps me forget the slaughter.' His face twisted in bitter recrimination. 'Poor excuse!

'What about you?' He suddenly turned the question on the girl. 'How did you end up in a town like Goldrush?'

Tallulah gave him a lop-sided smile, determined to

be as frank as he.

'I was an actress in a troupe that performed there for the miners. The gold rush was in full swing and we expected to make a killing.' She stopped to consider her story. 'I was called Josephine in those days, a silly little girl who'd run away from her respectable upbringing in St Louis to join a travelling theatre. I might have been well developed, physically that is, but I was an innocent abroad, or as innocent as a girl can be in such a troupe. I never did rise higher than singing and dancing in the chorus line, but I always longed for a principal role and when the showman took a shine to me I thought it would lead to stardom. It only led to his bed of course, and by the time we'd reached Goldrush I was tired of playing second fiddle.

'Jem Horne owned the saloon and was an important man in town, so I was flattered when he singled me out after our first performance.' She uttered a deprecative laugh. 'Not that he ever did, of course. I fell so violently in love I didn't even notice his other amours. I must have been blind! He was fond of me though; kept me with him when the troupe moved on and paid me to perform in the saloon to keep his customers satisfied. It was he who christened me Tallulah to deceive his customers into thinking they were watching a more exotic act.

'I was a fool; it took me a year or two to see what was under my nose, but I gradually realized that when he wasn't in my bed, he was in someone else's. Then, when I became desperate enough to face him with evidence of his infidelity, he just laughed in my face. We drifted apart after that, and it's been years since we shared a bed. I worked on in the saloon, I'd made myself too useful to be kicked out. I could still sing, though it's years since I danced, and I'd already taken over the chore of looking after the girls. I'd had enough of Jem, any man if it came to that, but the thought of moving on frightened me too much. I'd secured a place for myself in Goldrush. Not much of one, and it was a lonely life at times, but at least I didn't have to resort to selling my body.' She paused and stared at the scout with an air of wide-eyed confession. 'I wouldn't want you to think I was still the innocent young actress, there were always men willing to bear me company for a night, and I succumbed whenever the loneliness bore down on me too heavily.'

'If you weren't mixed up with Jem Horne's money-making schemes, why did you leave so suddenly?' Kit's question sounded more curt than he'd intended. He didn't want to hear about those other men. Since he'd taken to the bottle, no half-decent woman had so much as smiled at him until now. He was lonely too, and didn't want to believe he was just the next man in line.

'Jem told me he was selling up and urged me to fix my interest with the new owners.' She faltered. 'I knew what was expected of me, but I wasn't going to stick around and sleep with yet another man just to retain my position. I'd saved enough to move on and hoped to find myself a situation in some theatre.'

The girl stared down at her naked body and laughed harshly. 'I'm kidding myself again. That was Josephine's life, she would never have lain with a man like this.'

'She just has.' Kit rolled over and gently took the woman in his arms, kissing her with a tenderness that stirred her more than the violent love-making they'd shared so short a time before. 'Josephine,' he whispered into her receptive ear. 'I like the sound of it; it's a name that suits you.'

CHAPTER 9

BELINDA'S BETRAYAL

Once dark had fallen, Josephine and Kit restarted on their journey back to the Livingstone ranch. With the ever present risk of running into Pale Wolf or some of his braves high in their minds, they made slow progress with Kit scouting ahead on foot whenever the twisting trail looked ripe for ambush. While they remained in the shelter of the arid hills Kit travelled on foot too, leading the horse with Josephine on its back, but later, descending to the more open plain country, he rode tandem with her, deliberately holding the horse at a steady walking pace to conserve the animal's strength. If they came under attack, he wanted their mount to remain fresh enough to gallop under its double load.

By the time dawn broke they were once more

approaching the outskirts of the ranch, squatting under cover of a dried-out gulch from which the cabin could clearly be seen. Their horse had been tethered half a mile back to prevent it betraying their presence.

'There's no one left here.' Josephine stated the obvious, though the scout still engaged himself in minutely observing every inch of available cover.

'I believe you're right.' Kit was bemused. By all accounts Pale Wolf had escaped with the girl when he discovered his redskin brothers had withdrawn, but the remaining white men wouldn't have left the safety of the ranch. The stock had been run off by attacking tribesmen on the evening of their first attack, and without horses to ride it would have been madness to forsake the shelter of the cabin knowing there were war parties about, even if they weren't actually under attack. 'Stay here, I'll be back as soon as I can,' he ordered the saloon girl and began to creep towards the nearby ranch house.

'No way,' she told him curtly. 'I'll take my chances staying with you. If anything happened to you, I wouldn't last long on my own.'

This was so palpably true that Kit didn't argue and, with Josephine in his wake, he advanced on the cabin in a series of rushes, still attempting to use the natural cover of the land until they were within fifty yards of the ranch house. 'You were right,' he hissed at the girl, perplexed by the eerie silence that hung over the ranch. 'There's nobody around at all. No Indians. No guard on the cabin.' He pointed out the door that plainly stood ajar and rose to his feet warily. 'No one left inside either, I reckon. Not alive at any rate. Come on, we'll take a look.'

There was an all pervading smell of death about the open doorway, to which he crept warily, poking his head around its jamb with all the caution he might have applied in approaching a grizzly's den.

'About time you showed up.' The major's clipped accent greeted him, but the speech was made with an effort that matched the bloodless, death-like mask that suffused the retired army officer's face.

'Major, what happened?' Kit stooped down beside the officer who sat ramrod straight against the wall. 'No, don't talk,' he continued, appalled by the massive wound that split the officer's belly, staining the smart regimentals in a bloody red mess of gore.

'Got to.' The major's voice grew perceptible weaker while he spoke. 'I'll be dead soon; only stayed alive this long to testify against those rats. I knew you'd come back, whether you succeeded in your mission or not.' He coughed up some blood, but waved Kit back when the scout attempted to comfort him.

'It all started when that Indian of yours disappeared and took the saloon girl with him, may they both rot in Hell. He killed the sheriff too, cut his throat from ear to ear. We didn't even know they'd gone until I sent the sergeant up to spell them after Daniel Livingstone finally died. It was a bloody murder and I hope you make them pay for it. The sheriff was a good man.

'I said a few words over him then stood up top to search for sign of the Indians. It was too quiet for my liking, but no one was about, and neither did there seem to be an attack in the making. I guessed the devils had withdrawn for one reason or the other, but for what it was I never had the chance to find out."

'I was still out on the roof when the soldiers made their move. The sergeant had evidently reached the same conclusion as me and decided to take over before the red devils returned. I heard a shot, swiftly followed by a cry of pain, probably when they took out Jake. I leapt down through the skylight and found them waiting. The boy had a gun in his hand, but it was the sergeant who did for me. Caught me from behind while I was still recovering from my jump, sliced my belly open with that knife of his and left me to die slow.' The major coughed up a gout of blood and it was obvious to Kit he was nearing the end.

'The depraved bastards have taken poor Belinda with them,' the ex-army man told Kit, reaching forward to grasp the scout's hand in his agitation, 'but they'll likely kill the girl once they've had their way with her. Follow them. Don't let them get away with it.'

'They won't,' swore the scout, gently lowering the major's rapidly weakening body back against the wall he'd propped himself on.

'I don't know what happened to the band that attacked us, but I saw the half-breed again,' the old man made a final effort. 'He came back last evening.

I pretended to be dead, but he must have realized some of us were missing.' Kit cursed under his breath when the major stiffened. He felt for his pulse and stood up abruptly.

'He's gone,' he told the girl who'd been standing behind him.

'I'd wager Belinda's not been killed though,' Josephine told him. 'If she didn't plan the whole shebang herself in the first place, she'll have recruited the two of them to her cause by now.'

'She might wish she was dead if Pale Wolf's on her trail. No wonder he's not bothering with us any more. The carnage wreaked in here must have tipped him off to the truth.'

The pair saw to the grisly task of interring the inhabitants of the ranch house before they finally set off for town, still riding double.

'What do we do next?'

'Go back to town,' Kit told Josephine. 'What else? The answer to this whole damned mess has to lie in Goldrush. All the evidence points to the gold still being hidden in the saloon, or somewhere nearby at least.'

'Why the saloon? Surely there's too many people about to make it safe.'

'Gold's heavy in bulk,' the scout told her succinctly. 'Not easy to transport any distance on your own. Jem wouldn't have trusted anyone to help him, and handling draught animals or wagons would have raised suspicions, not to mention being easy to track. Besides, his rooms were over the saloon and he'd want to keep an eye on the loot.'

'I'll bet Belinda knows where it is.'

'Maybe.' Kit was still unsure. 'We know she was Jem's lover, but that's a whole lot different from trusting her with the location of the gold.'

'If Belinda was his accomplice, and all the evidence so far points to it, then she's the one killed him,' argued Josephine. 'She wouldn't dare do that without knowing where to search for the loot, even if she didn't know its exact location. I think the little bitch is guilty as hell. And there's another thing to think about: the sheriff's deputy will be in Belinda's pocket by now,' the saloon girl warned, in an abrupt switch of tack. 'She was affianced to him and she'll have invented a plausible story to explain herself, one that doesn't figure her as Jem's lover. He'll take her word against any suspicions we feed him. At the very least we'll be suspected of collaborating with the Indians, and we could even end up in jail!'

'You might be if you show yourself,' concluded Kit, giving Josephine's warning some thought. 'If she realizes you saw her leaving Jem's quarters early in the morning, Belinda must know you suspect her of being his lover if nothing else, but the last she saw of me I was risking my life to bring help along. So long as I don't turn up with you in tow there doesn't seem much reason to suspect me.'

The pair found themselves approaching Goldrush mid-afternoon, but the scout deliberately kept well away from the main trail that led into the town centre. Suspecting Belinda would be holed up some-where in town and not wanting to risk her seeing him in the company of the saloon girl before he'd had the chance to scout out the lie of the land, he doubled around the rear of the miners' shacks. From there, he led the tired horse on foot through the shaded, narrow back streets until he reached the tumbledown shack that served as his home.

'We'll leave the horse corralled out back here,' he told the saloon girl. 'If my story is ever going to be believed, I'll have to report to the sheriff's office first. His deputy will have to know about the raid in any case. In the meantime you could do with a change of clothing; that costume is barely decent.' He studied it with an interest that made her face burn, and amended his decision. 'In fact, it's positively inde-cent. You'll be arrested if you turn up dressed like that.'

'I left most of my wardrobe at the saloon,' Josephine replied archly, twisting her body to show off her figure the better for her lover's delectation. 'Jem said he'd get someone to send it on to me, but I doubt if he had time to do that. I can sneak in through the back way easily enough. With Jem dead I doubt if the saloon will be in use anyway.'

'Long as you keep out of sight until we know what Belinda's plans are. How do I find you?'

'Jem allowed me to use a room out back of the saloon,' she returned, and clung to him for a moment. 'Meet me there.'

*

The sheriff's office was closed when Kit reached it, the heavy wooden door locked, but the ongoing sounds of revelry drew him to the saloon only a few steps down the street. The scout wondered briefly who'd taken over from Jem Horne before striding purposefully through its doors.

When he entered all eyes focused on him and the hubbub audibly declined. Trail weary, ragged and dirty, he looked like a man with a tale to tell.

'Deputy,' he croaked, taking in the man wearing a star, 'there's been an Indian raid.' Then he opened his eyes wide with shock, feigning surprise at the sight of the woman next to the lawman. 'Miss Belinda, how'd you get here?'

In truth his surprise barely had to be feigned. He'd expected to meet the girl in town, but not acting as though she were the hostess in the saloon. Not only was she far too well brought up to frequent a place like that in such a blatant manner, he'd expected her to remain in hiding and await her opportunity to make off with the gold. Her gown was an eye-opener too; gone the modest, buttoned-to-the-throat costume she'd worn at the ranch, replaced instead by a brightly coloured confection tight enough to betray her figure and with a *décolletage* so low as to leave her breasts wobbling dangerously on the edge of indecent exposure. Not that the sight of her had taken all his attention. Josephine, dressed in no more than her petticoats, was standing behind, flanked by the erstwhile sergeant and lieutenant, both now dressed in civilian clothes.

'I've been promoted to sheriff since Miss Belinda reported Largo Baines's murder.' Ernest Clarke was too young to resist the opportunity to boast about his promotion, and he stuck out his chest to show off the badge. 'You're the guard off the stage, aren't you? Where the devil have you sprung from?'

'I've just arrived in town from the Livingstone ranch.' Kit stuck to the truth so far as Belinda would have known it. 'The stage was attacked by Indians and the survivors took refuge there. I managed to slip out to get help.' He stared helplessly at Belinda. 'What happened?'

'I could ask you the same,' she returned, with narrowed eyes. 'You went off to get help from the fort.'

'Indians got to the line shack before me, ma'am.' That much was true. 'Long way to walk and Goldrush was closer. Came to tell the story to the deputy and get me a horse.'

She smiled. 'No need to worry yourself any longer. Those of us who survived are safely back here in town. Have a drink instead.' She turned to the new sheriff and flung him a careless order. 'Take the lying whore away, you can put her in front of the judge tomorrow.'

To Kit's surprise, the young lawman reacted immediately to Belinda's command, leading Josephine away at gunpoint as though she, rather than he, was calling the shots.

'The woman betrayed us all,' Belinda told the scout, calling for a bottle with all the assurance of a woman who owned the bar. 'She and that Indian made a run for it a couple of hours after you left. They killed the sheriff and got away scot free while the rest of us fought off those painted devils. In the end we were the only survivors.' She pointed out her confederates who gathered closer.

'What happened to your uniforms?' Kit decided to put some pressure on the sergeant.

'Truth is we never were in the military,' admitted the big man easily. 'Took some uniforms off dead men in the hope we'd escape easier, but it didn't seem right to say that in front of the major.' He held out his hand. 'We didn't get properly introduced before. I'm Elmore Bunting and this here's Kansas. He don't have another name seeing as he's an orphan.'

Kit took the bigger man's hand, and once again felt the latent strength behind the firm handshake. 'You walked from the ranch house?'

'We were lucky,' admitted Bunting. 'Found some horses the Indians missed; out on the trail, mile or two from the ranch.'

Found some horses! Kit turned his attention back to Belinda before his face gave him away. There was a mystery there, but he let his eyes play over the lovely ranch girl, allowing his look of incredulity to be put down to her dress. She still had enough of her modest upbringing left in her to look sheepish.

'By the time we'd reached town my own clothes were in rags, so I borrowed some finery from one of the whores.' The girl explained herself without being asked, and carried on with a slight blush when the scout continued to stare at her neckline. 'I guess that sort of girl likes to put the goods on display.'

Kit raised his eyebrows. It was true that the women who worked the saloon weren't shy in showing off their bodies, but that didn't explain why a well-brought-up young lady should have eschewed the aid that would surely have been forthcoming from the more respectable matrons of Goldrush. He was more than ever convinced that the gold was hidden within the saloon and that it wouldn't be long before Belinda and her confederates shipped it out.

'The saloon's been closed since Jem died,' the girl continued her explanation, 'but the women were still carrying on their business out back. Fortunately the head barman had taken up a position behind the bar with a shotgun to protect the stock and it was he who suggested we take over. Elmore's had some experience of running a bar and we had nothing else to do, so we offered to manage the business until Jem's replacement showed up. Sheriff Clarke's been a dear, made it easy for us.'

I bet he has, thought Kit, remembering the way the young lawman had looked at the girl. 'What about Tallulah? What in the world made her go off with an Indian?'

'Why, she murdered Jem, didn't she? The sheriff would've taken her in as soon as we escaped. Nothing left for her but retribution. Besides, she's no better than a whore; apart from the chance to escape her fate, she probably wanted to rut with the filthy half-breed.'

103

'How was she caught? Did the new sheriff chase after her?'

'No, the most amazing thing happened. Kansas found her in her room.'

'In her petticoats?'

'She was changing. According to the kid her other dress was in tatters.' She turned for collaboration to the one called Kansas, and he nodded.

'I was waiting out back and saw her arrive. Didn't realize she'd killed poor Jem, but I sure knew about the sheriff and I thought I ought to bring her in for questioning.' Kit realized from the way he spoke the kid was acquainted with Jem Horne and began to wonder if the two of them were more than chance travellers caught up in an Indian raid. He decided it would be no surprise if they turned out to be co-conspirators.

'Funny you arriving the same time she did.' Elmore Bunting brought up the coincidence with offhand casualness, but Kit realized all three of them were waiting on his answer with too much interest for there to be any doubt. They had to be in the plot together!

'Be even funnier if her Indian friend was scouting around out back, too.' Kit pretended to misunderstand the question, but was agreeably surprised by the consternation his statement roused. Of course, if they were involved in the scheme to defraud the Indian chief, they must have realized by now that Pale Wolf and the half-breed who kidnapped the girl from the saloon were one and the same man. There again, the Indian was also seeking revenge, and it was all too likely he would be scouting around. Given the half-breed's savage reputation, it wasn't a statement likely to be welcomed by anyone who'd betrayed him.

Bunting looked as though he'd like to interrogate the scout further, but Belinda was running the show.

'You two have work to get on with,' she reminded the men. 'You know what to do.'

For a moment Kit thought Bunting might rebel, until he turned on his heels and strode off with the silent Kansas at his heels. Belinda was in charge, for now at any rate. Most probably, considered the scout, because she alone knew where the loot was buried.

CHAPTER 10

GUN FIGHT

'You're not leaving, are you?' Belinda laid her hand possessively on Kit's arm when he showed signs of drifting away. 'Stay for a drink. Please.' Her eyes opened wide in invitation.

Since the girl was his only clue to the gold, the scout had already formed the intention to stay as close to her as possible, but Josephine's arrest had changed his priorities. He didn't see what he could do to aid her in the short term, but neither did he intend to leave her to her fate without at least making sure she was as comfortable as possible. The young sheriff didn't look as though he'd make any push to alleviate the lot of an imprisoned saloon girl.

'Just one drink,' he temporized. 'I need a wash and change of clothes.' He batted trail dust off one arm of his jacket to reinforce his intentions. 'I'll be back later this evening if you're still around.'

'I intend to remain here until it's time for bed,' Belinda replied, when she poured a slug of rot-gut whiskey into his glass, but laid such blatant emphasis on the final word that Kit found himself shocked by her behaviour. The girl's strict upbringing, it seemed, had sloughed off as fast as her demure clothing.

'To later, then.' He saluted her with his glass and tipped it back, swallowing the stinging liquid in a single gulp, more to hide his surprise at her bold behaviour than in any need of the drink. Still amazed, he laid the shot glass back on the bar and strode out of the saloon without a backward glance. The girl had been coming on to him, but why? Did she suspect him of conspiring with Josephine? If so, to keep him under surveillance was the only answer that made sense. Her two confederates had been sent off to complete an already agreed task, but since they were still within the confines of the saloon mingling with the sparse afternoon custom, it couldn't have been to distract his attention from them.

Out on the boardwalk he shrugged his shoulders and forgot about the girl; he had better things to do than ponder on the imponderable. First, a wash and change of clothes, then a trip down to the jail. It would be pure foolishness to show any direct interest in Josephine's fate; if the sheriff suspected any complicity he could find himself under arrest too. Nonetheless, Kit intended to discover her circumstances by one means or another.

Though the scout did little more than sluice

himself down before dressing in clothes very little cleaner, if less obviously dusty than those he'd removed, the late afternoon sunshine was visibly receding into the gloom of evening by the time he exited his shack again. The light was still good enough, however, to clearly make out the slim figure of the kid named Kansas lounging against the wall opposite.

'Howdy.' The young hellion pushed himself away from the adobe building and stepped lithely into the narrow roadway to intercept the scout's progress. His stiff-legged posture, reminiscent of a coiled spring, was far more informative of his intentions than his attempt at a casual greeting.

'Howdy yourself.' Kit forced himself to remain calm and pretend he hadn't noticed the way the kid's hand was hovering over his gun. He had no intention of being diverted from his errand, and neither did he intend to take part in a gunfight that might bring a parcel of deputies down on his head.

'Sweet little package, that girl of yours.'

'Belinda?' For a moment Kit didn't connect the youngster with Josephine, or her predicament.

'The whore.' Kansas corrected his misapprehension, and tried to make the barb strike home, allowing his eyes to light up while he considered her charms. 'I wouldn't mind taking a tumble with her myself. She might be getting on in years, but she's hung on to her figure mighty well.' He grinned like a lad caught in a sweetshop. 'Watched her take off her dress an' all. Nice pair of tits and a nest of curls that'd test the preacher himself. Got myself a feel too, when I dragged her down to the saloon. How'd a bum like you manage to take up with a woman like that?'

'Fact is, I haven't. I only met her when she boarded the stage for Tuscatoon and I've not spoken to her since I left the Livingstones' ranch house couple of days ago.' Kit made an attempt to play down his involvement with Josephine, aware the other was only attempting to rile him into drawing on him in a rage. If nothing else it proved Kansas was a gunman sure enough of his speed in the draw to offer the scout the chance to go for his own gun first.

Kit's attempt at innocence on the part of the girl from the saloon failed as he'd half expected. Looking into the young gunfighter's eyes, he could clearly read there was no mercy on offer. They were dark and expressionless, the eyes of a killer, and the scout realized it wouldn't have mattered whether Kansas believed his story or not; he'd been sent out with instructions to kill.

'I think you're fucking her.' Kansas wrapped a smile around his face and went on as though his opponent hadn't spoken. 'Girl like that would rut with anyone.' The kid backed off a little to give himself more space when the fight finally erupted. He looked supremely confident and continued to needle the scout, though he must have been disappointed in his efforts so far. 'Probably went off with that Indian with the same thing in mind.'

'Give yourself a chance, kid,' Kit warned the

gunman, hooking his own right hand closer to his holster. 'Back off while you still can.' He was too experienced to let the youngster's words affect him and all too aware that his dishevelled and unshaven appearance gave the impression of a worthless drunk who'd be easy meat to a professional. In fact, as he ruefully admitted to himself, a drunk was about all he'd been the past few years, but, apart from sharing one whiskey in the saloon with Belinda, he hadn't seen a drink in three days and there was no longer any trace of alcohol-induced haze left to slow his own reactions. He was no fast-draw specialist, but he'd been brought up to exercise real skill in handling both handgun and rifle and was no slouch at either. Living most of his life with an ever present danger from relentless enemies by his side had honed those skills, and he would be no pushover, particularly if the cocky young gunman made the dangerous mistake of underestimating him.

'Take your own chance.' Kansas, confident in his own ability, attempted to stare the scout down. 'You can die with a gun in your hand like a man, or I'll shoot you down like the dog you are.' He cackled mirthlessly. 'You'll be joined in Hell by that whore of yours soon as the necktie party gets hold of her.'

'What d'you mean?' A sudden apprehension dawned on the scout about that little job for Kansas and Elmore Bunting. Of course, they'd been drumming up support for a lynching while Belinda kept him busy at the bar. With their plans so close to completion they couldn't afford to allow Josephine

110

to state her case before the judge next morning. That worthy might just believe enough of her story to make it impossible for them to escape with the gold without bringing further suspicion down on their own heads.

The kid cackled again. 'The townsfolk don't need much persuading to see a murdering whore hanged. A rope for her and a bullet for you. Miss Belinda will sure be grateful to me.'

'Did she send you?' Kit thought he already knew the answer, but the question might buy him more time and provide an edge. Kansas had all the appearance of a man who'd be lightning fast on the draw.

'Not her,' the other replied with a grin, confounding the scout's guesses. 'Reckon she's got the hots for you, but Elmore sure hasn't. Told me to gun you down. Make sure you were dead. We got our own surprise in store for that stuck-up little bitch once she tells us where the gold is stored.'

The kid's final evil laugh was his downfall. Kit drew and fired while Kansas was still gleefully reflecting on the pleasant prospect of taking Belinda down a peg or two. An expression of pure panic suffused the youngster's face for an instant, but his killer instincts rose rapidly to the fore, and within moments he'd launched his own swift reply, a draw as fast and sweet as any Kit had ever seen.

Too late! The young gunslinger had surrendered the initiative and duly paid the price of his mistake. The single shot was enough; the kid called Kansas was drilled through the heart and dropped dead

111

where he stood, his gun out and levelled, but not quite triggered.

Kit, no stranger to death, slipped warily into the sanctuary of the shadows and retreated rapidly down a convenient alleyway, heading swiftly away from the scene of the gunfight. The shot would bring the sheriff and his deputies running, and though there was not one in sight he knew the gunfight wouldn't have gone unnoticed. In any case, even if there were no witnesses willing to testify, he knew Bunting could be relied upon to cite him as the main suspect.

CHAPTER 11

JOSEPHINE IN DANGER

Kit wasted no further time before heading directly for the jailhouse. Josephine had to be sprung free if she wasn't to be caught up in a lynching attempt he didn't believe the sheriff would be man enough to halt. Not only that, her freedom was best bought while the sheriff himself was still engaged in investigating the gunfight that had resulted in the death of the kid. The lawman was under the thrall of Belinda, and he'd be anxious to see justice for any of her friends.

Common sense advised the scout to approach the jail more cautiously than the precipitate tack he'd taken to entering the saloon earlier. He hadn't expected to find Belinda in attendance there, and he didn't want to find any unpleasant surprises at the sheriff's office. That the sheriff and at least one of his deputies were looking into the shooting he already knew; he'd hidden in the dark depths of an alleyway while they ran past. How many other deputies did Sheriff Clarke have available? Not many, he reasoned, not in a town the size of Goldrush. Kit's own time in the caboose had acquainted him with only two others, but Sheriff Clarke may have recruited another in the wake of his own advancement, or even temporarily deputized an entire posse with the thought of an Indian war in the forefront of his mind.

It was getting dark and Kit was easily able to lounge in a back alley across the way from the sheriff's office, in the depths of which lurked the town jail, and study the place. There was, as he well knew, a small backyard, built to provide an exercise area for whatever prisoners might be incarcerated, though as far as his own knowledge went, never used for that purpose. The cells, four in all were built in a single row, each with a small barred window overlooking that yard, the entrance to which was a small door set so there were a pair of cells each side. Over the past few years he'd occupied most of these, and from his own observations he knew the wall enclosing the yard was both high and ringed along its summit with a fearsome barricade of barbed wire.

Ted Bateman was the only deputy in sight, standing a step or two outside the heavy office door and gazing up the street at a gathering crowd of rowdy men, illuminated by the light of their own flaring

114

torches. Kit's lips pursed in annoyance; the lynching party was gathering fast. Even at this distance he could hear Elmore Bunting's voice exhorting the men to march on the jail. He looked up and studied the roof line. The sheriff's office itself had a slight pitch; higher at the front of the building than the back, where the jail itself had been added on with a flat roof. Next door on one side was the saloon, two storeys high and flat-roofed; and on the other, a provisions store with accommodation above. That roof had a steep pitch with a dormer window inserted.

Deputy Bateman stepped inside the office, offering the scout a ray of hope he might be able to approach unseen, until this was dissipated by the man's reappearance with a shotgun under his arm. Kit approved; such a weapon was the only thing likely to deter a crowd intent on a hanging. Not that Elmore Bunting would be impressed, very likely he'd shoot the deputy down from the relative obscurity of the congregating group.

The lynch mob was moving, no more than a few yards at a time between swigs from the bottles that were being passed around, but they'd soon gather momentum. Not much time for the scout to contemplate rescue, but he slipped into the night, crossing the street on the further side from the crowd, unseen by the deputy who was watching the crowd with increasing trepidation. He ran along the back of the buildings, weaving between a jumble of the hurriedly thrown up shacks that housed the poorer elements of the townsfolk until he reached the jail.

The saloon would be too much of a risk so he turned his attention to the provisions store. There was a low built log store to its rear, and, following a quick glance around to check he was alone, he swung on to its roof. From there, a short scramble, aided by the sill of a barred and blacked-out window, saw him on the pitched roof and running adroitly along the edge of the pitch despite the danger of falling. A quick glance from his high perch showed him the lynch mob were closer now, and that deputy Ted Bateman had retired to the door of the sheriff's office, still with the shotgun prominently displayed.

He made a dive across the gap between buildings, landing with a heavy thud on the roof of the sheriff's office. He'd hoped his landing would be disguised by the angry roaring of the crowd calling for justice to be done, demanding that the filthy whore who'd traded guns with the Indians, killed Jem Horne and the sheriff should be strung up immediately. It wasn't to be; Ted Bateman looked up at the very same moment the scout made his second jump, directly over the man's head. Kit lashed out with the pistol he'd drawn in readiness and felt a satisfying thud as the man went down. Cat-like, the scout himself landed on his feet and dived into the office, slamming the door behind him and throwing the heavy bolts.

The lynch mob was scarcely slower. The bolder elements among it had seen the deputy go down and made a rush at the door, which was soon shaking in its frame. Kit knew he had only minutes before some-one thought to bring something heavy enough to cave the door in, and ran lightly across the room to the door that led into the cells. It was locked, but a heavy ring of keys lay in plain sight on the desk and he grabbed them, lucky enough to find the correct key on his third attempt. Josephine was the only occupant of the cells and Kit quickly ran across.

'What's happening out there?' Josephine, still dressed in only her petticoats, was pale with worry, and with good cause. She might not have realized the full horror of her situation, but the lurid shadows thrown by the flaming torches and the crashing of fists on the office door had alerted her to the possi-ble danger.

'Just one or two of our good citizens,' Kit told her easily. 'Belinda's organized a necktie party for you.'

What blood was left drained out of Josephine's face. 'Get me out,' she wailed. 'Quickly.'

'Damn these keys.' Kit had quickly seen that four similar keys had to belong to the cells, but he'd tried all but one before he found the correct combination. 'Out back,' he called to the girl and began to work through the remaining keys to discover the one that opened that last door. By this time the thudding fists had been joined by the heavier crash of a battering ram, and the door, heavy as it was, was beginning to splinter. 'Come on,' he cried, when the way to the backyard was opened. 'Up you go.'

He made a step with his interlaced fingers and when the saloon girl inserted her foot, boosted her up to roof level. In a flurry of lace and athletic limbs she clung on and heaved herself over the edge. Kit followed, pausing only to relock the door through which they'd just passed, knowing the lynch mob would be on him in a few seconds more.

'We'll have to jump for it,' he told the girl, who was looking around the small roof space in dismay. Suiting his action to the words he leapt the alley to the pitched roof next to it and clung on. For a brief moment he began to slide, but quickly caught himself and beckoned to the girl.

She shut her eyes and made the leap into his arms. 'Are we safe?' she whispered into his ear, flattening herself against the steep tiles.

'No,' decided the scout. 'Not for long. They'll be through the back door soon and it won't take them long to work out which way we went.' A thunder of feet below them justified his words. 'They're surrounding the place now.'

He raised himself into a crouch and began to tow the girl up the steep pitch. 'We've got to be away from here before they climb on the roof themselves. There's a window around front, we'll enter the store through that and sneak out as soon as we're able.'

In fact their escape was achieved in a far easier, if somewhat scarier manner. The front of the building was reached without mishap, but the slope here, and especially around the dormer window was much steeper than at the back. Josephine's feet slipped first, and her frantic grab at safety took the scout with her. Once on the move, nothing could stop their tumble and the two of them went over the edge two storeys up. Kit's arm flailed as he made a desperate grab at supports for the sign the advertised the store's business, and for a moment Josephine hung, a dead weight in the crook of his other arm. The support gave and they dropped again, landing in a jumble on the boardwalk in front of the store, but the momentary respite given by the check in their fall saved them from serious injury.

Only a few of the more timid members of the lynching party had remained out front while the action was going on inside and behind the jail, and they quickly scattered when Kit drew his pistol and loosed off a few rounds over their heads.

'Come on,' he cried, and towed Josephine at full speed into the jumble of back alleys that led behind the respectable façade of the main street. It was a world he knew, and he unerringly worked his way towards the livery stable.

'Whose horse is that?'

'Damned if I know.' He was damned if he cared either; their own case was too desperate to wonder about someone unknown's reaction to a missing horse. Reaching the relative safety of the dark depths of the stables Kit had merely drawn out two likely horses at random. Now he was busily engaged in saddling them while Josephine watched the street. The livery boy wasn't in evidence either; he'd joined the lynch mob, or was watching events from the side-lines. Kit didn't care which so long as he stayed away.

'Horse theft is a hanging offence, mister. If you live that long!' The first either of them knew of Elmore Bunting's appearance was when a light flared through the darkness and he spoke.

Kit reacted immediately. He saw the lantern and shot it out. Bunting cursed angrily and tried a shot of his own, but the scout had already moved, raced across to the door and spinning Josephine around and into cover.

'Where the devil did he spring from?' he murmured into her ear. It was a rhetorical question and he didn't expect an answer, which was just as well since Josephine had none to give.

'Better come out, Kit.' Belinda's voice joined that of the big man. 'The mob will be around to investigate the shooting soon. They're in an angry mood, and there's no need for you to die as well as her.'

'Not likely!' Kit doubted Elmore Bunting would allow either of them to live, mob or no mob, but he said no more. The devil of it she was right; the lynching party, or some of them at least, were bound to follow up on a shooting. The sheriff too, if it came to that. Unless they lit out within the next few minutes their escape attempt was doomed.

He tried a new tack. 'Once he's through with us, Bunting will get rid of you too. The kid told me they planned a double cross once you'd led them to the gold.'

'Don't listen to him.' Elmore Bunting betrayed his position and Kit loosed off another shot, hoping to get lucky, though any shooting was a lottery in the dark depths of the livery.

'I'm not a fool, Elmore. Just get them before anyone else finds us.'

'Too late, Belinda.' Sheriff Clarke's voice rang out from the door, where he suddenly appeared, outlined by what little light was provided by the rising moon. 'I'm already here.'

'Ernie.' Belinda's voice rose in pitch, but she swiftly regained her nerve. 'Help us, we've got those gun runners bottled up.'

'How much did you hear, Sheriff?' Kit voiced all their concerns. Though there'd been no admission of guilt from either Bunting or Belinda, their words had to throw some doubts into the man's mind. If he'd heard them!

'Enough to realize you're all as guilty as each other.' Sheriff Clarke wasn't mincing his words. 'Thieves and killers, fighting amongst themselves. Now throw down your guns and step out into the open where I can see you. You'll all be up before the judge in the morning.'

'Damn it, Belinda.' Elmore Bunting swore out loud. 'I told you we should have done it my way in the beginning instead of trying to charm the snotty-nosed little bastard.' He fired and Sheriff Clarke paid the price of allowing himself to be backlit. He fell with a cry.

Kit shot again, aiming at the flash of light emitted by the gun, but there was no evidence he'd hit his target.

'Get into cover, Sheriff,' he called anxiously, sensing the lawman was on the move, and afraid the man would expose himself again. 'Bunting's a killer from way back, and so's your lady friend.'

'I guess you're on the level after all, Kit.' Ernie Clarke dragged himself further into the barn; his wound was serious enough to prostrate him temporarily, but he didn't think it would prove fatal.

'Too right, Sheriff.' Kit squirmed on his belly and rolled desperately across the floor before the sound of his own voice gave away his position, but no shot rang out from the outlaw duo.

Damn, he thought. What were they doing?

CHAPTER 12

BELINDA'S STORY

Kit shifted his position again, slipping noiselessly towards the sheriff's location. He didn't speak until he could hear the breath rasping in the other's throat.

'Are they still there?' he whispered hoarsely.

The sheriff whirled around with a gasp of surprise. He hadn't heard the scout's silent approach and Kit felt a moment's fear the lawman might actually open fire on him. 'Jesus Christ, Kit, I damned near shot you down. It is you, isn't it?' Sheriff Clarke was beginning to feel he was too inexperienced for his new position; too damned jumpy under fire. His wound was bloody painful too. 'I haven't heard a damn from them in ages. Have they gone?'

'I believe so. I haven't caught sight nor sound of them since they opened up on you.' Kit was still concentrating all his senses into the darkness where he'd last seen the pair of miscreants. If Belinda and her sidekick had managed to escape, they'd been mighty quiet about it. They hadn't used the main entrance either; he'd have spotted their silhouettes outlined against the night sky. Nevertheless he couldn't detect their presence and since they hadn't arrived via the big barn doors, with time slipping away, he made a deliberate decision. Straightening up in a single lithe leap, he raced precipitately towards the last position he'd marked them, gun up and ready to shoot the instant he came under fire.

There was no one there, but a previously unsuspected side door opened on to the alleyway that ran along the side of the building and he realized they must have slipped through immediately after shooting the sheriff.

'OK, sheriff,' he called. 'They've gone.'

'Thank God.' The sheriff gamely attempted to stand on wobbly legs, but was only too pleased to rest his weight on Josephine's shoulder when she rushed forward to support him once she'd been reassured their enemies had departed.

'We'd better get after them before they get away with the loot.' The scout was already carefully peering around the open door, ready to take cover on the instant if the escaping duo had set an ambush.

'Ernie Clarke's going nowhere until he's seen a doctor,' Josephine replied for the sheriff while she gently lowered him to the floor and calmly lit up a lantern. 'Took a slug in his shoulder by the looks of it. I don't think the wound's life threatening, but it's

124

bleeding hard. You'd better fetch help before you do anything else.' Kit turned to watch while she curled up beside the pale-faced sheriff and drew his head down on to her lap.

'You'll see the girl remains safe?' he spoke to the sheriff for confirmation.

'I'll see to it,' promised that worthy weakly. 'Guess I was a fool to believe the story they concocted anyway.'

'Probably,' Kit agreed easily. 'Would have fallen for it myself if I didn't know the truth. Guess most every-one else in town was fooled by her as well.' He turned and slipped out of the stables to fetch Doc Gray, all too aware that Bunting and the girl would be using the time they'd gained to make their escape. However galling, the sheriff's need for doctoring had to come before any attempt to corner the two miscre-ants; not only did common decency demand it, but he was also the only one who could vouch for Kit and Josephine's innocence and the other parties' guilt.

Once the doctor had been alerted, however, Kit set his mind to accomplishing his other pressing mission. The missing pair would no doubt be plan-ning to make their getaway with the gold while the town was still in such a kerfuffle and the scout intended to put a spoke in the wheels of their plan, whatever it was. The saloon would be his first port of call, but first he had to evade the cheated lynch mobs roaming the streets. They'd be looking for Josephine primarily, but he wouldn't have put it past Elmore or Belinda to have put it about that Kit himself had broken the girl out of jail. Consequently he made slow time.

At last he had the building in sight, not from the main street, but behind, where a jumble of near derelict shacks spread their deep shadows to hide his presence. He could hear the sound of a piano playing above the hubbub at the bar and there were lights showing at several windows, but the only ones he was interested in were upstairs. He'd never been invited on to the first floor of the saloon, but he knew that apart from guest and reception rooms, Jem Horne had an office up there and presumably his own rooms too. He was betting on the office being at the front of the building, and acted on his assumptions immediately.

Breaking in was easy. The saloon girls had their quarters at the rear, and unless they'd scored with one of the customers they'd be touting for business in the saloon proper. One window stood wide open, no more than a few feet above Kit's head, and having listened carefully for the give-away sounds that might indicate one of the girls was entertaining a client, he swung easily on to its sill. It was too dark to see inside, but the utter silence within confirmed in his mind that he was entering an empty room, and a moment later he'd emerged into the long corridor that served all the rooms and led eventually into the main bar. He had no intention of betraying his presence by entering the saloon proper from which the main staircase ascended, but sought instead a subsidiary stair which he was sure must exist.

It did, and a minute or two more saw him sidling up to a door that was slightly ajar, a sharp wedge of light escaping from its portals. The slight figure of a girl paced up and down within. Kit eyed her figure suspiciously, but she was alone and didn't seem to be armed, so he seized the chance and entered.

'Where's your accomplice?'

Belinda whirled around with a cry of alarm. 'You,' she gasped, and raced behind a magnificent desk that dominated the room. A pistol lay on it in plain sight, but although she managed to lay her hands upon it, Kit was on her before she could level the weapon. A cruel twist and she dropped the weapon again, crying out in sudden pain.

'Don't even try to escape,' Kit ground out the threat as he whirled her away from the fallen hand-gun, but still keeping her wrist imprisoned in his own firm grip. 'Where is he?'

'I'm here!' A second door opened at the far side of the room and Elmore Bunting strode in with the pistol in his hand firmly pointed at Kit's midriff. 'Move away, girl. It's high time I did away with this rat.'

'Don't be a fool, Elmore.' Belinda angrily wrenched her wrist away from the scout's weakened grip. 'Any shooting up here will bring half the town down on us, and who's to say the sheriff hasn't got his deputies out already. We'll tie him up and gag him. Jem always kept a supply of rope in that cupboard over there. Use some to bind him.'

That Bunting wasn't pleased by her intervention

127

was obvious, but neither could he deny the truth in what she said. 'You heard the lady,' he offered mockingly and indicated a chair set in front of the big desk. 'Get yourself sat in that. You, girl; keep him covered while I tie him down.'

Belinda picked up the pistol she'd so recently dropped and trained it on the scout while Elmore withdrew a length of rope from the cupboard indicated and used it to truss Kit with casual skill. The scout used all the tricks he'd learned to make securing him difficult, but Elmore Bunting knew them too, and circumvented every attempt to leave a knot looser than it should have been. He drew back, content with his work at last and stood in front of the scout with a satisfied smirk on his face.

'The kid will sure be pleased to see you like this,' he taunted the scout. 'I sent him after you, but I guess the stupid little bastard lost your trail.' He smiled, an evil grimace that totally failed to reach his eyes. 'He'll sure be hot to find your girl too, may even be with her now. I doubt if she'll like that; Kansas can be real mean around women, especially those who reject him. He has a way with that knife of his to change their minds.'

Since Kit knew the kid was dead, Bunting's barbed taunts failed to hit home in the way the outlaw had hoped.

'I doubt if he will,' the scout drawled contemptuously. 'Not unless she's in Hell as well.'

'What d'you mean?' Elmore Bunting looked put out.

128

'If we're talking about Kansas, he found me. We shot it out before I broke the girl out of jail. He's dead.'

'Damn. I thought he could take you too.' Elmore Bunting looked at the scout with a new respect. 'How'd it happen?'

'Maybe he could have taken me,' asserted Kit, 'but he was too busy boasting what a big man he was. Let me get the drop on him.'

'That's Kansas all right. Stupid to the very end.' Elmore Bunting uttered a short, sharp laugh, but there was no humour in it. Abruptly the expression on his face changed to one of fierce hatred and he raked the scout with a back-handed swing that nearly took his head off and spilled the chair and its contents across the floor. 'He was useful to me, even so.' The powerful outlaw followed up with a kick aimed at the scout's ribs that he could barely block by shuffling around the floor on the upset chair, but nonetheless grunted in pain when it connected on his thigh. Thwarted, the big man stepped around and aimed another kick at the scout's ribs, which if he'd connected as he'd planned would certainly have broken two or three.

'Stop that.' Belinda didn't demur while he stuck to abusing the scout with his feet, but her voice rang out peremptorily when Elmore Bunting drew his gun. 'Fire that pistol and you'll bring the deputies down on us. They'll know by now exactly what we're up to and, worse still, that you shot him.'

'Maybe he's dead.' Bunting's voice took on a sulky

tone and he kicked the scout's chair viciously.

'Forget him. The gold's hidden under the floor-boards in Jem's bedroom. Down the corridor, last door on the right; search under the bed and you'll see where they've been taken up recently.'

'What about him?' The big man stared at the scout hungrily, the blood lust still on him.

'Just leave him; he can't interfere while he's trussed up in the chair. I'll stay and watch him.' She casually picked up the pistol from the table, where she'd dropped it during her struggle with Kit, and leaned back against its solid bulk, levelling the barrel in direct line with her prisoner's head.

Elmore Bunting's face still held a measure of disquiet in its expression, but he strode out of the door on his mission without another word. Belinda gave him a minute's start before she too stole across to the opening and peered suspiciously down the corridor.

'He's gone,' she announced in satisfied tones.

'What I told you in the barn: it's true. He's planning to double cross you once he gets a hold of the gold,' Kit started his offensive with a statement calculated to alarm her.

'Of course.' Belinda didn't seem unduly surprised. 'Why do you think I didn't tell him or his partner where the gold was hidden earlier? Jem never trusted them either, but he needed their help to float the scheme.' She yawned in a gesture intended to dismiss the men. 'He always intended for us to give them the slip once we'd smuggled the bullion out of the territory.'

'Why did you tell Bunting where the gold was just now?'

'To get rid of him.' Belinda curled up on the floor by Kit's head. Not only was her skirt shorter than she'd normally wear, it was slit up one side, and she deliberately allowed the full length of one shapely leg to protrude, bared from ankle to high on the curve of her thigh. 'I still need someone to help me get the gold out,' she purred, 'and Elmore Bunting's not that man.' She smiled alluringly and hooked up her leg to allow her toes to massage his thigh. 'There's a fortune waiting for us to take it. You don't even have to work at loading it on the mules; Elmore's doing that right now. We could be good together. Forget that dance hall cutie of yours; Jem Horne did, and he never regretted it.'

'Never regretted it!' Kit's voice rose incredulously. 'You killed him for it!'

'Not me.' The girl made the denial sound like the truth. 'It must have been Elmore or the kid. I loved Jem; we were due to go away together and make a new life for ourselves. Life's too hard for a woman out here in the West; Mama always told me so, and she was right. She was going to return to the East as soon as Papa died, but she didn't have enough money of her own to give us any sort of life. Jem's scheme to defraud the Indians would have seen to that.'

'How did a girl like you meet a man in his position?'

'Jem met a lot of women.' Belinda sounded defensive until she gave a little giggle. 'I surprised him once with the mayor's wife. They made me promise not to tell anyone.' Jem Horne's reputation with the women was a byword in town, and it didn't surprise the scout he'd had an assignation with the mayor's wife. 'He sought me out later, told me how lovely I was. It's lonely up at the ranch, and no man ever treated me like Jem. Or made me feel like a woman. Not even Ernie, who was going to marry me. Guess I was ripe for the plucking!'

'You became his lover?'

'Every chance I got. I even started to use the old line shack as a retreat, telling my parents I needed some time to myself. Then every evening I'd ride down into town to spend the night with him.' She huddled closer to Kit, using her body shamelessly to seduce him to her side, and ran her hand tenderly down his cheek. 'We could be like that, if you've a mind to.' She allowed her face to hover closer to his own while her hands eagerly searched his body. 'I can feel you want to.' Her soft lips closed over the scout's.

'What the hell!' Elmore Bunting had reappeared in the doorway, staring at her in dumbfounded amazement. The expression on his face told them both he'd been listening long enough to form an opinion on what they'd been talking about. 'I'll kill the pair of you,' he ground out and began to advance on them.

'That's far enough.' Belinda rose gracefully to her feet and levelled her gun on the angry man.

Stymied, he could only stand helplessly, menaced by the unwavering barrel of her pistol.

'Why aren't you loading the gold?'

'You know why, you double-crossing bitch.'

The girl tightened her finger on the trigger in a deliberate motion intended to frighten the big man into an answer. 'I asked you a question. Tell me, or I'll shoot your balls off.' The barrel dipped towards its new target and the big man paled at the determination on the girl's face.

'The gold isn't where you said it was. I pulled up the floorboards under the bed and there's nothing there.'

'Fool. You got the wrong place.' Belinda took a couple of steps towards the door in an immediate and miscalculated reaction to the unpleasant news before she realized her danger. She caught herself abruptly and tried to retreat, but Elmore Bunting seized on her mistake while she was still unbalanced. He flung himself on her, knocking her pistol hand down, and grappled at close quarters, relying on his greater strength to subdue the woman.

She was as much aware as the scout that her life depended on the outcome, but overborne by the other's bulk could do nothing to help herself. Still struggling wildly the outlaw pair crashed to the floor in a deadly embrace and the pistol went off with a muffled crack. Several seconds passed before the scout was able to discern which of the suddenly still forms was the one hit, or even if the bullet had by some strange means killed the both of them. Then the girl gave a hideous howl and pushed the dead weight of her attacker off her. She stood up, still shuddering in the grip of a deadly fear, then looked down at the spreading bloodstain on her dress. 'Oh, my God.' She tried to brush it away, but only succeeded in staining her hands with the viscous, scarlet fluid. 'Is he dead?'

Kit stared at the silent figure laid out on the floor. 'I guess so,' he confirmed. Bunting didn't appear to be bleeding, but he certainly wasn't moving and the blood on Belinda's dress wasn't her own. 'Get me out of these bonds and I'll take a closer look.'

'Will you help me get away?' Belinda made a conscious effort to bring her seething emotions under control.

The scout grinned and winked at her. He'd seen just what was happening behind the girl's back. Josephine was in the doorway, though she didn't appear to be armed. 'Lay that pistol down and kiss me properly. I'd do anything for a sight of those legs again.'

Belinda grinned triumphantly. She laid the pistol aside and stooped to kiss the bound man, saucily allowing the skirts to peel away from her legs.

Josephine pounced.

CHAPTER 13

JOSEPHINE TO THE RESCUE

Belinda had been taken unawares, but she wasn't going to give in without a fight. Josephine had attacked her with one arm around her throat in a stranglehold and hung on to the hand nearest the gun that still lay where the girl had put it a short time before, but that left one arm free and the ranch girl used it to good effect. Arching her body, despite the way it constricted her breathing even further, she caught hold of the heavy desk and used it as a fulcrum to magnify her strength.

The newcomer sailed over her shoulder in a froth of the petticoats which were still all she wore. Belinda followed on when the stranglehold was suddenly broken, lashing out with doubled fists at her opponent's face, when she should have been taking advantage of the saloon girl's temporary daze to retrieve her pistol. A moment later it was too late and the women closed again.

They were a well-matched pair, of similar size and weight, and if the girl from the ranch was younger and in better condition, then it was matched by the saloon girl's fierce ruthlessness, born from years of experience staying on top in the rough-house tumble of a saloon. For several minutes they milled about the floor, their skirts flying wide in a whirling display of lace and trim curves, the younger girl lashing out with pugilistic skill while her opponent fought to stay in close proximity where her cat-fighting abilities could be made to tell.

Eventually, sensing her opponent was far from happy throwing punches, Belinda attempted to rise to her feet and keep the fight at a distance where she could use her fists to advantage. Josephine, however, was having none of this. Rolling with the punches, and making no attempt to regain her feet, she squirmed close enough to seize the younger girl's hair and wrench it painfully. It brought a satisfyingly pain-racked shriek, so she followed up in an attempt to bite her ears, only desisting when Belinda stooped down to her own level and sank her teeth into the gleaming alabaster skin of the saloon girl's shoulder where the yoke of her petticoats had slid down her arms. She jerked away, tearing her bloody flesh from between the other's jaws, then bore back in, her fingers still fastened painfully in Belinda's hair. Shaking her like a dog, and ignoring the shrieks and unladylike oaths that sprang from the ranch girl's mouth, Josephine attempted to twist the girl around to tumble her beneath her own body weight.

Unable to escape from the pain engendered by the furious pulling of her hair, Belinda forged a primeval response; fighting, scratching, biting what ever part of her opponent she could reach. Her questing hands, seeking to scratch out the older woman's eyes, caught instead a hank of hair and began to yank on it fiercely, howling in triumph when Josephine was forced to let go of her own. She pressed forward, certain that victory was beginning to run her way. Her other hand caught in the flailing petticoats, tearing and rending at the lacy garment until she screamed out in jubilation when the material began to rip.

Josephine hadn't been top dog in the saloon for nothing however. She'd seen the girls fight and ignored the sensation of having her clothes ripped apart where she lay. Her own fingers bunched in the bosom of Belinda's dress and tore it open, the cheap dance-hall costume coming apart at the seams and peeling away to bare the ranch girl's pert little breasts. Gasping with indignation, the girl attempted to pull the material back around her form, only realizing too late how that reaction opened her defences to the other's advantage.

With a tiny cry of triumph, Josephine lurched forward and tumbled the girl under the weight of her body, hanging on desperately while her opponent threw herself into paroxysms to throw off her

enveloping weight. A moment of quiet while the
ranch girl garnered the final reserves of her strength
saw the older woman avail herself of the chance to
throw her legs either side of her opponent's body
and straddle her. By now in total command,
Josephine sat astride the half-naked beauty and
pummelled her face with doubled fists. Belinda
desperately redoubled her struggles in response,
writhing and arching her body to throw off her
nemesis, but her efforts were to no avail: the older
woman held the advantage and she had no intention
of surrendering it. Her fists thudded again and again
into the unfortunate girl's face, or sank painfully into
her bare breasts while she clamped her thighs
around her opponent's body to hold on to her position on top. Abruptly the fight left Belinda as she
succumbed to exhaustion and the continual drub-
bing, and she could only wail numbly while
Josephine continued to slap her furiously around the
face.

At last the older woman was satisfied the girl would
be unable to offer her any further resistance, and
crawled off her still body. Gasping for breath, shaken
and badly beaten herself, it took a moment or two for
her to pull herself together and gather up the pistol.

'Good girl,' Kit told her, 'but you'd better release
me before she recovers.'

Josephine obediently sank down beside the scout
and pulled at his bonds distractedly, swearing
coarsely when she was unable to move them.

'There's a knife at my belt,' he told her. She

fumbled around his waist for the weapon and a moment later he was free to take her into his arms, where she promptly burst into tears in a stark reaction to the savage fighting that had seen her win through victorious.

'Let me see to your face,' he offered, knowing she was still in a daze from the fiercely fought contest. Bending low, he wrenched a hank of material off the ruined bodice of Belinda's dress and began to wipe away some of the blood. 'You're going to be badly bruised,' he predicted, taking charge of the pistol, 'but none of the wounds is any more than superficial. Let's get this girl on her feet and look for that gold.'

'You know where it is?' Josephine's startled query hung in the air.

'Yes. Under the floorboards in Jem's bedroom. Bunting couldn't find it, but Belinda was quite sure that was where Jem hid it. He must have been looking in the wrong place.'

'Fair enough.' Josephine nodded with what sounded like a sigh of relief, and taking a fistful of Belinda's hair, drew her to her feet. Totally ignoring the younger girl's howls of pain, she then took a firm grip on one wrist and twisted it behind the girl's back. 'Come on, you little bitch; show us where this loot of yours is buried.' She pushed the girl towards the doorway despite the way she staggered unsteadily on her feet, callously controlling her by means of the painfully pinioned arm.

'Please.' Belinda, bent double by the ferocious grip, attempted to beg, but elicited only a laugh from

139

the older woman who carried on driving her, utterly unsympathetic to her discomfort.

'Let her be,' demanded the scout shortly.

'Do you think she'd take it easy on us if the tables were turned?' Josephine cried, and twisted the poor girl's arm higher, laughing again when Belinda suddenly realized how she was displayed and tried to use her free hand to cover up her breasts with the remnants of her bodice.

They entered Jem's bedroom together and stared at the destruction wrought. The bed itself had been roughly tipped against one wall, the bed-covers strewn all about, while where it had once stood the floorboards were in disarray. Kit approached and stared down between the beams. There was nothing there.

'Was this where the bed stood?' he asked the ranch girl.

Still dazed, she could only stand and stare, but Josephine was having none of this. Dropping her painful grip, she swung the girl around and slammed her against the wall. A moment later she let her have it; her open palm slapping the girl's cheek in a round-house swing. She set herself again, but Belinda wasn't even going to attempt denial.

'Yes,' she cried, wincing away in case the blow was followed up. 'The bed was there, honest it was.'

'And the gold was stored underneath it?'

'Yes. Jem reckoned that was the safest place for the loot. While he was awake he could keep an eye on it, and when he was asleep any thief would have to disturb him to get at it.'

'Figures.' Kit stared at the empty space under the boards. 'Only it ain't there.'

'Shall I beat it out of her?' Josephine looked as though she'd be only too pleased to put her suggestion into action, and the ranch girl cringed away, uttering a terrified moan deep in her throat.

'No,' Kit decided. 'She's telling the truth. You can see she's as shocked as we are by its absence. In any case, she'd already told Elmore Bunting this was the place. Someone must have moved it; probably the same person as killed Jem. Find them and we'll find the gold.'

CHAPTER 14

LAST THROW
OF THE DICE

Pale Wolf dropped in with a suddenness that took them all by surprise. Just where he'd come from wasn't clear, not that it mattered. In a trice he'd seized Josephine in one strong arm and hauled her in front of him to protect his body, while the other hand held a large hunting knife on Belinda, where the unfortunate girl was still slumped against the wall following her interrogation at the older woman's hands. Her head snapped back against the wall in alarm, her vulnerable throat open to the bright steel, stained with the slow trickle of blood from a barely felt nick, a monument to its razor edged sharpness.

'Let them loose.' Kit raised the pistol in a deliberate movement, hoping the threat would be enough to gainsay the Indian chief.

142

'No.' The half-breed spoke in guttural English while he tightened his grip on the girl from the saloon who was showing signs of restlessness. 'There can be no justice for Pale Wolf from either the red man or the white now. I'll kill them both before I surrender.'

The scout calculated the odds in his mind with swift deliberation. He had enough confidence in his skill with a gun to believe he'd be able to hit the Indian if he fired; probably even kill him, though he suspected that Belinda at least would lose her life. Josephine too, if the first bullet failed to kill him outright.

'What d'you want?' he asked at last, knowing a stand-off was inevitable. Unless he was pushed into a fire fight, he couldn't take the chance with the lives of two women at risk.

'Lay down your gun.'

'No chance.' The scout knew all their lives would be worth nothing if he gave up his advantage.

'I'll slit this woman's throat,' offered the half-breed easily, nodding towards Belinda, who moaned in fear, and was only prevented from cringing away by the sharp steel caressing her neck. The slightest of moves from his knife hand and another bright ribbon of scarlet ran over her pale skin.

'If you're after the gold, then she's the only one who might know where it is. She's Jem Horne's partner.'

'She was,' agreed Pale Wolf, displaying a knowledge of the situation far beyond that of the scout, 'but we cut her out.' His other arm shook the woman in his embrace to leave no doubt about where he thought the answer lay.

'She has no idea—' Kit's protest was cut off short when the Indian began his explanation.

'Belinda was part of the original scheme. I knew them all. The other three are dead already and, when it suits me, she too will die for betraying me in front of my people. My stock amongst the tribes suffered badly when the guns didn't appear, but at least I knew where the gold was and promised to return it, together with the bodies of those that would double cross us. Jem Horne was their leader and I went to him first, but the woman was already there, arguing with him. Once it became clear he had no intention of providing the guns or returning the gold, I killed Horne and made her help me to hide the loot in a place I could bring back braves to remove it later.'

'When I returned the following night the gold had gone from that place. The one they call Tallulah in the saloon must have moved it, for she was the only other who knew where it was hidden. There was no time to seek her immediately, the tribes didn't believe me and were out for my blood. I escaped with what few followers I still had and sought her on the stagecoach.' He growled deep in his throat. 'Even those few have left me now, for which I have you to thank.' His voice almost broke with the pain of his next confession. 'Since I lost the prisoner I can no longer live with the Indian, but to live like the white

144

man I need money. The gold is mine by right, and I intend to take it.'

'The sheriff will come eventually,' Kit told him. 'You can only hold the women so long.'

'I am content to die,' admitted Pale Wolf, 'if it may be in battle. They will die with me.'

'Then die like a man. A brave.' The scout made his final calculation, knowing it was the only way to save the women's lives. 'Fight me man to man, and show me how an Indian chief should die.' He threw aside the pistol and plucked his knife out of its scabbard.

For a moment the Indian chief looked startled, then smiled wolfishly. He threw Josephine aside as easily as the scout had dropped his pistol and removed the knife from its position at Belinda's throat. The exhausted and frightened girl slumped wearily to the floor, utterly worn down by her beating and the fear of Pale Wolf's vengeful knife.

'Prepare to die, white man. Your soul will gain from your bravery in facing me man to man.'

Kit suspected his soul would do no such thing, but he didn't tell the Indian that, preferring instead to take stock of the man he was about to fight. The scout already knew Pale Wolf was a big man, but facing him at the point of a knife he somehow contrived to look even bigger; heavily muscled too, but for all that light on his feet. The half-breed too studied his opponent; the white man was the shorter by an inch or two, but broad. At any other time he might have thought him flabby, but the Indian had already seen for himself the feats of which Kit was capable, and had no intention of underestimating the scout's ability.

Suddenly the play began. Pale Wolf danced forward on nimble feet and feinted to draw his opponent in, knowing he was the younger by several years and could expect to hold the advantage in staying power. It didn't surprise him when Kit evaded his first lunge with ease, the feint was never meant to strike, but only to provide information on how well the white man could handle a knife. The riposte was expected, but not the dazzling speed of it and the Indian leapt nimbly back with new respect in his eyes.

For several minutes the two well-matched opponents circled warily around each other, one or other of them occasionally launching an abortive attack, probing for a weakness or following up where the other had left himself open for the merest fraction of a second. They were fighting for their lives, and both of them knew it; though each might respect the other's ability, neither was willing to offer quarter. It would be a fight to the death.

Kit brought the first phase of the fight to an end, closing with his enemy to test his strength. He knew enough about the half-breed's speed and ability with the knife to realize that a prolonged fight would provide a test for his stamina, a test it might not pass. Not only was he older than his mighty opponent, he'd spent too much time at the bar in recent years to be considered fully fit.

Pale Wolf sliced back-handed when the scout bore

in and knew a momentary satisfaction when a bright band of blood opened along the white man's forearm, but it was a fleeting feeling. Kit seized his knife arm and attempted a riposte of his own; an underarm lunge that would have ended the fight there and then if the Indian hadn't managed to sweep it aside with his own free arm. The scout reversed his grip in the wink of an eye, and drove his point back at the half-breed's ribs, a scything attack that the Indian did well to avoid. Then Kit's wrist too was held in his opponent's fierce grasp.

The two men struggled backwards and forwards, each trying to break the other's hold in order to utilize their weapons again, but for several long, muscle-straining minutes neither could gain an advantage. Kit ached in every part of him, and he knew he had to pull something out of the bag before the Indian's greater store of stamina proved the break-through each desired. He dropped to one knee, hoping to throw the other off balance, but though Pale Wolf's grip was for one vital moment loosened, the Indian hung on grimly and the moment passed. The scout was now on the defensive; on one knee he was forced under the half-breed's weight, who now could bring all his vast strength into play.

Kit took a chance and, dropping his own hold on the Indian's wrist, rolled rapidly across the floor. Pale Wolf cursed and struck, but in the sudden, unexpected twist, he'd lost his own equilibrium and the stroke had no force or accuracy to it. The scout escaped with no more than a flesh wound to his shoulder which didn't bother him at all. He struck back and for the first time his blade thrust home, slicing open a cut on the other's chest while he rapidly back-pedalled, still off balance. The white man followed up his advantage immediately, his flickering knife point driving the half-breed before him.

Pale Wolf wasn't finished yet, however. Recovering his balance with an effort, he launched a fierce attack, throwing up one arm to take the full force of Kit's slicing blade, while he attempted a lunge to the scout's belly. The white man leapt back to avoid it and circled slowly, taking stock of their new situation. The Indian's arm had taken a jagged wound that clearly bothered him in exchange for the abortive stabs at his opponent's stomach. The odds had changed dramatically, but Kit knew full well the fight was far from over when he drew back to assess the situation: the half-breed was still a dangerous opponent.

The shot startled both men. Kit's eyes flew around to stare at Josephine who was holding his pistol in both hands, the barrel smoking slightly where the shot had left it. Pale Wolf, also, turned his head towards her, but he dropped his knife and clasped his chest too. The scout turned his attention back to the Indian when he sat down heavily, too badly wounded for his legs to support him any longer, a whoosh of shocked breath leaving his body. Josephine fired again and he dropped to the floor, clearly dead with the side of his head shattered.

148

The scout staggered forward, but Josephine menaced him with the gun. 'Stay where you are.'

'It was you all along. Why?'

'A girl has to live.'

'But—'

'I found out what was happening the day Jem died. He was still fond of me and called me into his office to tell me he intended to sell up and leave town. He thought I'd be all right if I made up to his successor, but I'm too old to go through that routine again. I knew there must be something behind his leaving and it didn't take much to wheedle the story out of him. Jem always was too vain for his own good and he soon told me how clever he'd been. He'd already betrayed Pale Wolf and was planning to do the same to his other partners.'

'Not me.'

The other girl's interruption had surprised Kit who'd almost forgotten she was there, but Josephine favoured Belinda with a caustic glance. 'You too,' she confirmed. Her voice rose. 'You stupid slut. Did you really think you were the only woman in his life? You were just a convenient body, not even a particular favourite.' Her eyes raked the ranch-girl's figure derisively. 'It was all a game to him. To corrupt your innocence was his idea of fun, but once you'd given in to him he soon lost interest. He'd have dropped you if it hadn't been for the gold; he couldn't run the risk you might tell anyone about it.' Turning her attention back on Kit with a final sniff of disdain she continued her story.

'It was the wrong time for Jem to boast about his dealings with Pale Wolf. The Indian chief had sneaked up the back stairs to check up on him and overheard the whole sordid story. He already had an inkling that Jem planned to double cross him, but once he knew the full details he was an angry man. He flew across the room with a knife in his hands, and although Jem reached for his gun, he was no gunman and the Indian was on him before he pulled it. There was a flurry of blows before Jem dropped to the floor, while I stood rooted to the ground, too frightened to even call for help.

'Pale Wolf stood over the body, his knife dripping blood, and glared at me. I knew I was next in line and opened my mouth to scream, but before I could make a sound he was across the room with his knife at my throat. I froze again, desperate and willing to do anything to save my life. Luckily I knew about the location of the secret place under Jem's bed; he'd used it to hide his belongings for years, especially those he didn't want others to see. I told the Indian about it; I was gabbling, but luckily he understood my meaning.

'I think he still intended to kill me, but first I had to help him with the donkey work. Moving the gold to a new hiding place, one where the Indian braves could sneak in undetected late at night to spirit the treasure away. It's not a huge undertaking, but there was more than one man could comfortably smuggle out of town, especially an Indian. Fortunately he was a man as well, and I sold my body as the price of staying alive. When he left me it was with a promise of what he'd do to me if I betrayed him to the authorities in town.

'I had no intention of bringing in the authorities though. I booked my ticket out of Goldrush and spent most of the night moving the gold to a new hiding place. I'd find an innocent accomplice to pick up the gold later; all I wanted was to be well out of Pale Wolf's reach. Somehow he heard of my flight and discovered I'd moved the gold. Hence the attack on the stagecoach.'

Josephine smiled reminiscently. 'You were closer to the truth than you realized when you rescued me from his camp. Pale Wolf already knew his time was over and he'd taken off his braves on a wild goose chase so he could come back on his own and force the truth out of me. I gave you a pointer in Belinda's direction and before you could mull things over and see the flaws in my story, transferred your thinking from your head to your pecker.' She grinned at the expression on Kit's face. 'Don't be angry with me, Kit; it was fun for us both, wasn't it?'

She gave the scout a coquettish smile. 'I'd like to repeat the experience; I'm sure you would too. Perhaps we can make love in a big, soft bed as a celebration after we've converted the gold to cash. I still need an accomplice to help me get it out of Goldrush.'

'I've seen what happens to your accomplices.' Kit was confident he'd become surplus to requirements as soon as the loot was safely out of Goldrush if he agreed to the saloon-girl's terms.

Josephine shook her head sorrowfully and care-fully lined the gun up on Kit's head, still trying to justify herself. 'I'm sorry you feel like that, Kit. We would have made a good pair, you and I.'

A shot rang out.

Josephine staggered and abruptly sank to her knees. 'You bitch,' she hissed at Belinda who was holding a tiny handgun. She tried to line up her own pistol on the girl, but no longer had the strength to aim it properly. Kit kicked it out of her hands just as she collapsed completely and told Belinda to fetch the sheriff.

'Are you crazy?' Belinda held the gun loosely, but it had two barrels and only the one had been fired. 'Nothing can save her now and I have to get away from here; out of town, anywhere.' She began to work on pinning up her ruined bodice to provide the barest semblance of modesty. 'The others are all dead and gone. Why should I be the one who stays to face the music?'

'Because you're the one who threw in with Jem to sell guns to the Indians. You could've started a war that would have killed hundreds of innocent settlers if the plan had gone through.'

'Oh, no,' Belinda denied the charge emphatically. 'We always planned on a double cross. There's not a jury on the whole frontier would convict me on account of plotting to defraud a two-bit Indian who's not even a proper chief. I'd be sitting pretty if

Bunting hadn't gone off half-cock; *he's* the one started the killing. Even then there's no proof I was involved, save in shooting the sheriff down at the livery. Ernie won't let me off on that count; we were engaged and I took against him.' She sighed. 'He'll be mad as a hatter when he realizes I was Jem's lover too; I always kept him at arm's length like a good girl should.'

'What about all the others you killed?'

'As I said, Bunting's work. I kept you alive, didn't I?'

Kit knew Bunting would probably have killed him if she hadn't intervened Not that he intended to admit to it out loud, she'd saved his life for her own nefarious ends.

'How d'you intend to escape without money?'

Belinda strode across the room, keeping a watch-ful eye on the scout, and shifted Josephine's still body with her toe. To Kit's surprise the woman stirred and emitted a moan of pain. 'She's still alive, just. We could make her talk.' She put everything into a pleading look. 'If we had the gold you could come away with me. I need a man I can depend on.'

'No one's going anywhere,' the sheriff spoke, from the door. His left shoulder was tightly bandaged, but he held a pistol in his right hand, and it didn't waver from the ranch-girl's figure.

'Ernie!' Belinda threw him a glance. 'Don't shoot, please.' She let her gun hand drop, still loosely hold-ing on to the little derringer. 'I would have married you,' she wavered, taking a stumbling step in his direction, 'but you don't know how hard life is for a woman out here in the West. Without money, and you just a deputy.' Her voice began to wheedle. 'You do still want me, don't you?' Her free hand had been fiddling with her bodice and it dropped to expose her breasts again.

The sheriff stared, distracted for just long enough for her to launch the attack. The small gun swung in a blurred arc that connected with his temple and dropped him to the floor. Another arc and it spat fire, the bullet barely missing Kit's head when it thudded into a beam close by his form.

He raced forward, but the girl had gone and he was brought up short by a moan of pain.

'Sheriff,' he gasped, and dropped to his knees beside the inert form.

'Damn her,' Ernie Clarke swore. 'I'd wanted her for so long, and there she was for the taking. No wonder I was distracted; my own fault. Get her for me, Kit. She'll have to stand trial and take her chance.'

Kit's first thought was for Josephine, rather than catching Belinda. The girl had nowhere to run to, not now she'd abandoned the gold.

'How is she?' Clarke asked, when Kit squatted beside the wounded woman.

'I think she's dead,' Kit replied with a tinge of sadness in his voice. When his fingers failed to detect a pulse, he leaned forward to listen for the beat of her heart. 'Dead and gone,' he confirmed. 'Gold's gone with her; if she hid it too well for Pale Wolf to detect, I reckon no one will find it.'

'Damn the gold. Get Belinda. If she tries to make a run for it, those Indians will kill her for sure.' The sheriff attempted to struggle to his feet, but sank back down with a groan and buried his head in his hands.

CHAPTER 15

CHASE

Kit headed for the livery. There were two horses already saddled there and, what was more to the point, Belinda knew about them. If she was going to attempt an escape from Goldrush that's where she'd be. If not, then she could be anywhere, probably close to the saloon; unless she'd discovered Josephine's death, she'd still have her sights set on the gold.

The livery was still empty and, more importantly, the two horses were still where he'd left them, fretting under the weight of their saddles. Knowing it was only a matter of time before he tracked the girl down, he took the opportunity to return them to their own stalls before he made his way back to the saloon.

Close by, he took cover in the dark alleys surrounding the building and settled down to wait. There was a window he'd broken himself and he suspected it would prove a magnet to the fleeing girl. Somehow she'd have to get to Josephine if ever she expected to get her hands on the gold. It was a long wait and he wondered if he'd called it right.

An hour passed before he heard the sheriff on the street. 'Damn you, Doc, I'm fine. Just let me speak to my deputies before you shoot me full of laudanum.'

Kit's ears pricked up; the saloon would be empty and if Belinda was truly about, this would be her opportunity.

It was, but not only her opportunity. The girl made directly for the broken window, only to find four shadowy forms rising up from her very feet. One grabbed the girl, muffling her distraught attempts to cry for aid with his hands, while the other three closed around them, rifles at the ready. This was no time to launch a rescue attempt and the scout settled for following the strange procession through the slums towards the nearby creek.

Belinda struggled, but her feeble strength counted for nought against that of the Indian brave who held her. One of the others scouted ahead, while the remaining two took up a position in the rear, striding crab-wise with their rifles very much to the fore. No chance for the scout to intercept them and he knew it.

They'd have ponies waiting on them up the creek and he circled warily around the slowly retreating group, judging their direction to show him whether their animals were tethered up or downstream.

He raced off, but no luck there, either. Two more

Indians were on guard, alert enough to warn the scout that any attempt to creep up on them would inevitably take longer than he had. Even as he made the decision, he could hear the abduction party approaching. Belinda had been gagged, but further off from the main streets the Indian warriors felt brave enough to dispense with their quiet retreat and take the remaining distance at a run.

They laughed harshly and thrust their frightened prisoner forward, though none of them dropped their guard for an instant. Another push and the girl fell, only escaping a hurriedly thrown kick with an agile twist of her lithe body.

Kit pursed his lips and set off at a run back towards his own shack. His mount would be rested, and he'd be able to follow Belinda's captors. Perhaps they'd become careless once they'd left the town well behind.

This time when he mounted the horse he had taken from the Livingstone ranch, it was saddled. He expected a long ride in the wake of the braves; long enough to take him deep into Indian territory at the least.

They were gone when he arrived at the creek, as he'd known they would be. Even though it was still night, with only a faint moon to light the scene, the tracks were plain to be seen in the soft ground down by the water's edge. A pile of clothes told its own story, and even before he'd picked them up to examine them, he knew they were hers: a torn, shoddy dress, and various pieces of lacy frippery just like she'd have worn beneath it. The warriors had stripped her where she lay in the sand. He cast around at the signs and pieced together the story, using his tracking skills and imagination with equal facility.

They'd attached a lead rope to her, probably about her bound up hands, and tied her to one of the ponies. Their trail lead off into the night and he followed slowly. They'd started off slow, probably still watching for any sign of pursuit from the town, but forced their mounts into a trot further off. Kit could see where Belinda had been forced to open her stride to match their speed, and once or twice the impact of her fall where she'd scraped along the ground before managing to regain her feet.

A mile or two out of town and he found the gag, no longer needed in the vastness of the plains. There'd be not one to help the girl out here! And that was where they'd ended the matter; revenge in its most vicious form. Still attached to the horse she'd been forced into a full out sprint to keep her feet, not withstanding that she'd already be exhausted by her enforced march at speed. A few yards later she'd hit the ground; he knew their play, they'd removed her gag to hear her scream.

If he read the sign correctly, again and again they'd allowed her to gain her feet then galloped her off them and dragged her tortured body across the rough prairies. At last she'd no longer been able to rise and Kit knew he'd be seeing the bloodstains if it hadn't been so dark. She'd soon be dead meat and he began to cast about.

Despite his skill at tracking it was almost an hour before he found her grotesquely mutilated and hardly recognizable body. She'd suffered horribly, but must still have been alive when they finally brought the game to a halt, for her throat had been laid open from ear to ear. He turned away sickened, and wished for a moment he'd mounted a rescue bid back at the creek, though he knew it would have been useless. Even if he'd had a dozen armed towns-folk at his back, they'd have killed the girl before she could be rescued. As it was he'd been alone and they'd have killed him for sure, or captured him to join Belinda on her final journey, at the end of a rope behind an Indian pony.

He dug a grave and thought for a moment of pursuit, but he'd already lived a life of revenge for the death of his father, and that had brought him no peace. Instead he said a few words over the pitiful grave, mounted up and rode hurriedly towards town.

Goldrush was his home. If he recovered the lost silver from the wreck of the stage he might be allowed to take Jake's place as the stage-line's repre-sentative in the town. Or perhaps to take his place at the bar again!